MW01137091

WRONG

Jana Aston

R~x~ **WRONG**

By Jana Aston

Reader:

Prescription:

Dr. Lucas Miller
BALDWIN MEMORIAL HOSPITAL

Dedication

This book is dedicated to Kristi Carol for putting up with my insecurities all year. Beverly Tubb for loving the first draft more than I did. And Julie Huss, without whom this book would never, ever have happened.

One

"Sophie, your favorite customer is here." Everly snaps a towel on my ass and grins at me.

"Everly, shut up! He'll hear you."

Fuck, I'm already blushing. Luke. He comes into the coffee shop every Tuesday morning. It's the highlight of my morning shift at Grind Me, a coffee shop just off campus. I work around my classes at the University of Pennsylvania. The Grind Me location I work at caters mainly to professionals and students living in off-campus apartments.

Luke definitely falls into the professional category. I'm not sure what he does, but he strolls into Grind Me in very expensive-looking suits and sharp ties. Nothing like the college boys in athletic pants and graphic-print tee shirts. He must be ten, fifteen years older than me. It doesn't matter. He's beautiful and I have a bit of a thing for him, which is bad because I have a boyfriend. An age-appropriate boyfriend. But it's just a harmless crush, right?

But Luke… he makes my panties wet just ordering coffee. He's tall, over six feet by my estimate. Thick dark hair, brown eyes and eyelashes any girl would kill for. He's wearing a dark gray suit today with a plum-colored tie. Fucking swoon.

His hands, I'm a little obsessed with them. Long fingers ending in short, impeccably clean nails. They just look... capable. I have a lot of fantasies involving his hands and my body. He's gotta know what he's doing with those hands. I bet he could get me off in minutes— those perfect fingers would know just where to curve while his thumb pressed down on my clit. He could probably make me come one-handed while he finished a phone call on his cell with the other.

I have a lot of fantasies about Luke based on nothing more than pouring him a cup of coffee every Tuesday and ringing him up. Always cash. I have no idea what his last name is. I wouldn't even know his first name if I hadn't listened in to one of his calls while he pulled a twenty from his wallet. "It's Luke, tell Dr. Kallam it's urgent, I'll hold."

Unfortunately, I don't think my fantasies are returned. I don't think he'd even know my name if it wasn't stamped in bold on a pin stuck to the front of my apron.

"Sophie." He always addresses me by name. *Good morning, Sophie. I'll have the dark roast, Sophie. I think you have a bit of whipped cream on your nose, Sophie.* That stuff splatters, okay? "Sophie?" Oh, shit. Has he been talking to me while I fantasized?

"Sorry! Um, daydreaming." He smirks at me. Bastard. "Large dark roast?"

"Please." He slides a five-dollar bill across the counter. "Have a great day, Sophie." He smiles again as he turns and strolls out of the shop. I watch him walk, free to eye-fuck him without being caught. The door jingles shut behind him but I keep watching until he's out of sight.

"Whew, that was hot." Everly fans herself with a takeout bag. "Sexual tension. Is it warm in here?"

"Stop it."

She loves teasing me. We go through this every week. He must hear her snickering in the background. And she ensures I'm the one who waits on him every time. If she's at the counter when he arrives she immediately finds something else to do so she can step back and watch me ogle him. It's embarrassingly obvious.

"Enough of the mysterious hottie. Are you going to put out and fuck Mike or not? You've made him wait like, a month? That's a long time in horny college-boy time. Plus, you're the oldest virgin on campus. Not even our campus. All the campuses."

"It's not my fault I dated a gay guy for two years." I tuck a strand of hair behind my ear and cross my arms across my chest. I'm a little defensive about this.

"Hello? Earth to delusional. You didn't find it odd you were dating a twenty-year-old guy who never tried to stick his dick in you?" Everly dumps beans into the industrial-sized grinder and raises a skeptical eyebrow in my direction. I hand her a stack of one-pound Grind Me bags labeled for individual sale and lean against the opposite counter.

"I thought he respected me, not that he was afraid of vaginas," I tell her, kicking the rubber mat on the floor over an inch. "He let me suck him off." I add this in, hoping it's a valid point in my defense.

Everly snorts. "Yeah, with the lights off."

I bite my lip and look away.

"Oh my God! I was joking. I'm so sorry, Sophie. Shit, seriously? Guys love to watch themselves get sucked. But

Scott was probably picturing a dude while his dick was in your mouth, so… Oh, fuck. I'm making this worse." Everly drops the coffee bag under the dispenser. Beans scatter across the counter and drop to the floor while she grabs me into a giant hug. "Lots of guys would love to fuck you, Sophie. I promise. Like Luke. That guy would love to stick it in you, he's just concerned you're jailbait. But you should start with Mike anyway. Tall, dark and handsome looks like he's packing a donkey dick."

"You've got a really charming way with words, Everly. You should write a book or something." I break out of her hug and grab the broom to sweep the coffee beans off the floor.

"Anyway, it's a go with Mike, right? Just get it over with. Mike will do, he's hot. I'd fuck him."

"Everly!"

"I wouldn't do him without a condom though. Safety first. And tell me you made an appointment with the student clinic. You should always have two forms of birth control, because I'm not ready to be a grandmother." Everly hops up onto the back counter and watches me sweep. "You missed a few to your left."

"Everly, you're twenty-one and we're not related. You wouldn't be the grandmother."

"Whatever. Semantics."

"That's not what semantics means. What are you majoring in again?" I glance over as she swipes a muffin from the bakery case and peels the wrapper back.

"I'm majoring in Professor Camden," she replies around a mouthful of muffin. "Which is better than this muffin. Jesus. Who pays for this crap?"

"Not you, clearly," I observe as she tosses the muffin

into the trash. "Yes. I have an appointment at the clinic today after shift. I shaved my legs and everything." I pull an elastic from my wrist and gather my long brown hair into a ponytail before bending down to sweep Everly's mess into a dustpan.

"What about your vagina? Did you shave that?" Everly reaches back into the bakery case and extracts a brownie covered in caramel.

"Noooo," I respond slowly. "I don't think the gynecologist will expect me to be bald. Right?"

"Holy fuck. This brownie. Now this is good. Orgasmic good. How much are we charging for these things?" I'm guessing she doesn't care because she doesn't stop talking or check the shelf tag for a price. "Oh my God. Do you want a bite?" I shake my head no and she continues.

"I can't wait for you to have an orgasm. Not a brownie orgasm, a penis orgasm. Which you won't have this weekend unless Mike is really, really talented. Which he's not old enough to be, trust me. But that fucker better make you come with his tongue or fingers before he sticks it in you. 'Cause that is not going to feel great the first time or two. So yeah, Mike might want you bald. I'll hook you up with my girl Leah. Her waxing skills, amaze."

She drops the half-eaten brownie on the counter and pulls her cell phone from her pocket while I'm distracted with a customer. By the time I finish making a medium vanilla hazelnut latte and turn back to Everly, she's finished her phone call and gone back to devouring the brownie.

"You're all set. Thursday. I texted you the address.

You're welcome."

"Everly! I never agreed to get waxed."

"Don't be a pussy. The gynecologist is more uncomfortable than a waxing. You're going to love it, trust me. The friction is so much better during sex. God." She smiles. "Plus even in your jeans. I swear you're going to be horny all day Friday with your bare vagina rubbing against your jeans."

I shake my head. "This conversation is so wrong."

"What are you girls talking about? Naked pillow fights at the dorm?"

"Shut up, Jeff." Everly doesn't even look up from her brownie.

"You can't speak to me that way, Everly. I'm your manager, it's insubordination." Jeff is a senior at the university, just like we are. His father owns this little chain of coffee shops and gave Jeff this one to manage.

"You can't sexually harass us either, yet you do. Why don't I conference-call your daddy and we can discuss my sexual harassment lawsuit while you lodge your insubordination complaint?"

"Fine," Jeff mutters. "At least get off the counter. And write down all the food you steal on the stale list. My inventory is always off when you work." He turns around and heads back into his office. It's not really an office, it's a desk he set up in the stock room—complete with an executive chair he picked up at Costco one weekend, dragging it through the back door like he was setting up shop to run a small empire, not manage other college students at a coffee house.

Everly hops off the counter muttering under her breath. "That guy's got a future ahead of him. In middle management, where he'll motivate no one and annoy everyone."

"He's not that bad, Everly." She gives me a look that says she disagrees. "Okay, he is that bad," I agree.

"Truth." She goes back to filling the one-pound bags of coffee and thankfully drops the topic of waxing. I'm not sure I intend to keep that appointment. The one I have later this morning is enough to think about.

Two

The rest of my shift passes in a blur of lattes, iced mochas and a steady stream of both commuting students headed to campus and professionals headed to nearby businesses. After clocking out I make my way to the nearest bus stop on foot. I have less than an hour to make my appointment at the student clinic and I don't want to miss it. Condoms are easy enough to get, but getting a prescription for birth control requires an appointment and an exam, and if I miss this appointment there's no telling how long it will be until the next opening.

The university has a shuttle system that loops around the campus, but Grind Me is several blocks outside the transit loop, hence why our undergraduate student customers are few. It's cool outside with fall well under way and I wrap my jacket tighter around me as I hustle to the bus stop, grateful that a bus is pulling up just as I arrive. The buses run every fifteen to twenty minutes so I'm glad to have caught this one.

The shuttle bus is fairly empty, it being late morning. Students are already in class or still sleeping. The clinic is only a few stops away on Market Street, between my Grind Me stop and my dorm. I've only used the clinic once before, freshman year, when a case of strep throat made its way through half my dorm.

It's quiet when I arrive, the receptionist looking bored while a couple of students wait for appointments, passing the time on their smartphones. She hands me a clipboard filled with forms and instructs me to complete them and sign every page before bringing them back to her.

I take a seat and hurry my way through the questionnaire. Name, student ID, phone, allergies, medications, family medical history, date of last period. Still less invasive than an average shift at Grind Me with Everly. The thought makes me smirk. I finish and slide the pen under the clip before returning the entire thing to the receptionist and sitting back down to wait.

I'm relieved when a nurse calls my name moments later. Hopefully this will go quickly and I'll be out of here in the next half hour with a prescription in hand.

The nurse is a friendly-looking woman with a big smile wearing zebra-print scrubs who tells me to call her Marie. She starts chatting the minute I'm through the door, leading me to an exam room where she gets my weight and blood pressure before explaining that I will need to remove all my clothing including underwear. I'm not sure who attempts a gynecologist appointment with their underwear on, but I don't say anything.

"What brings you in to see the doctor today, Sophie?" Marie peers at me over her clipboard, smiling kindly. I bet her grandkids love her. She's got three. They spent the weekend at her house and wore her out. She's told me all about it while taking my vitals, gesturing and laughing at their antics.

"Birth control. I'd like to get on the pill." I try to sound confident, despite my embarrassment at speaking about my potential sex life with her. She reminds me of my grandmother, the woman who raised me. My mom had me her freshman year of college and died before I was two.

"Good, you're a smart girl. It's always wise to take charge of your birth control." The nurse nods approvingly. "Have you been to a gynecologist before?"

"No."

"Well, then you're in luck. We have Dr. Miller on Tuesday mornings. He's the chief of obstetrics at the hospital, but he volunteers here a few hours a week. Otherwise you'd be stuck with one of our general practitioners and they're not known for being gentle. I'll give you a minute to undress and then I'll be back with the doctor."

The door closes behind the nurse with a whoosh. I quickly disrobe, tucking my bra and panties between my shirt and jeans, as it seems rude to leave them visible. I slip the dreaded paper gown on and hop onto the table. Shit. My socks. Marie didn't mention socks. I wish she had. Underwear I know I have to take off, but socks? Is it weird if I leave them on, or weird if I take them off? I'm still debating when there's a knock on the door asking if I'm ready. Socks on then, I guess.

The door swings open and Marie walks in.

With Luke.

Coffee-shop Luke.

The suit jacket he was wearing this morning is gone, replaced by a white lab coat. The plum-colored tie I was so enamored with just a couple of hours ago is still knotted firmly around his neck.

Oh my God. My fantasy crush is a gynecologist. *My* gynecologist.

Three

"You okay, sweetie?" Marie shuts the door and pulls a tray of instruments next to the exam table. "I told Doctor Miller it's your first time, he'll be gentle."

My face must betray my mortification. I look at Luke. I thought he hesitated when he walked in the room, but now he's giving nothing away.

"Sophie"—he glances down at his chart—"Tisdale. Miss Tisdale, I think we've met before?"

Am I having an out-of-body experience? Can this moment get any more embarrassing? He doesn't even know where to place me outside of the coffee shop. The guy I have fantasized about every Tuesday for weeks is now my gynecologist, and worse—better?—he doesn't know who I am.

"Grind Me," I blurt out. Oh my God, stupid coffee shop name. "The coffee shop, Grind Me." His expression never changes.

He glances back down at the chart in his hand. "Undergraduate, twenty-one." He trails off, his finger tapping the underside of the clipboard. Damn him and his attractive fingers. He flips a couple of pages on my chart. "You wanted a prescription for birth control?" He looks me straight on and my heart rate skyrockets. This is not how I imagined having his undivided attention.

"Right," I reply.

"Have you given any thought to what form of birth control you'd like? The pill is a pretty convenient choice for women your age. I could give you an IUD, but I don't recommend them for younger women who haven't yet had children. There's a patch and ring, they both have pros and cons as well."

"Just the pill," I interrupt him. "The pill is fine."

"I can't stress enough that you need to practice safe sex and use a condom in addition to the birth control pill, unless both you and your partner have been tested and decide to take that risk."

"Okay, I will."

He pauses. "You will or you do? It only takes one time, Sophie." He's washing his hands in the small sink along the wall, then turns back to me as he dries his hands on a paper towel. "Are you currently sexually active?"

"Um, no."

"So no sexual contact in the last four weeks?"

"Um, no. I've never had sex."

He pauses for a second then, his eyes moving from the paper towel in his hands to meet mine. "Okay, then." He shakes his head a little and tosses the paper towel into the trash. "We'll start with a breast exam and then do the pelvic. I'll get a swab for a pap smear, though I don't anticipate any issues. The clinic will call you within a week if there are any abnormalities." He glances at the instrument tray. "Marie, can you get me a small speculum? I assume you have some here." Marie pops up from her position on a stool by the door and leaves the room.

Once she's gone Luke looks at me again. My hands are folded in my lap and I'm swinging my stupid sock-covered feet off the end of the exam table while he runs a hand over his jaw.

"I can reschedule you with another clinic doctor if you're not comfortable, Sophie."

I'm not comfortable but I blurt out, "I'm fine!" Admitting I'm uncomfortable would be even more uncomfortable.

Luke flexes his jaw and rubs the back of his neck. It occurs to me now how stupid my fantasy crush was. This is the longest amount of time I've spent with him, and the only time without a counter separating us. Still, I can't help being attracted to him. I know it's wrong. Fucked up. Delusional. I'm already wondering if my future career will pay enough to cover the therapy I obviously need.

Marie is back and places something wrapped in heavy-duty plastic on the tray. The object makes a thud as she sets it down before taking up her seat beside the door again, sticking her face into an old copy of *Good Housekeeping*.

"Lie back on the table, Sophie." Luke's face is unreadable as he walks over to the exam table. He wraps a hand around my wrist and raises it over my head, his eyes passing over my face briefly before he sets my hand on the table.

His fingers move to the gown covering me. *Do not be turned on, do not be turned on, do not be turned on*, I chant to myself. I snap my gaze away and focus on the ceiling.

There's a motivational poster on the ceiling right above the exam table. I burst out laughing just as I feel

Luke's hands on my breast.

"Sorry, are my hands cold?"

"No, your hands are perfect," I blurt out without thinking. I think I detect a slight smirk on his face before I revert my gaze to the poster on the ceiling.

"The poster." I gesture upward with my free hand. It strikes me funny that there's a motivational poster on the ceiling. Like that's gonna take my mind off where I'm at. Or is it meant to motivate me to stay on this table? I giggle again. Luke tilts his head and looks at the ceiling.

Shit, are my nipples hard? That's normal, right? He's not doing anything erotic, but his hands are on my breasts. Yeah, my nipples are hard. His fingers are flat against the sides of my breasts now. He's rotating them around in what feels like a spiral pattern before lightly pinching my nipple. I have to stop myself from moaning a little. His hands feel good. I'm sure they're not supposed to, but they do. Luke slips the paper gown back over me before moving around the table to repeat the process.

I should probably stop thinking of him as Luke and start thinking of him as Dr. Miller. I stifle another giggle. I thought he was a banker or a lawyer in his expensive suits and trendy ties. Freaking gynecologist. Not one of my Luke fantasies ended like this. Yet, maybe they should have. I'm oddly turned on right now.

Chief of obstetrics, Marie said. Which would make him a surgeon, I think. So I wasn't wrong about him being good with his hands. I think about how many times I've masturbated pretending it was Luke touching me and I feel a rush of heat between my legs. Wrong. This is so wrong. Who gets aroused during a doctor appointment?

Luke is snapping plastic gloves onto those perfect hands. They're dark blue, which catches my attention. Aren't medical gloves always white on TV shows? Why am I thinking about this now?

"Sophie, I need you to slide to the end of the table and place your feet in the stirrups."

I glance over at Marie. Her nose is still stuck in *Good Housekeeping*. I scoot to the end of the table and wonder if I'm wet enough for him to notice. Is there a normal amount of wet for this situation?

"A little more, all the way to the edge. That's good."

My heart is racing now. He may be hot, but this is beyond awkward. I place my feet in the stirrups and lie back. My hands are clasped below my chest and I start twisting my fingers. It's too quiet in this room.

"So you're the chief of something? At the hospital? The nurse mentioned you're only here on Tuesday mornings."

He pauses. "Yes. Chief of obstetrics."

"So you do surgery and stuff? When you're not volunteering at the free clinic?"

"Yes, Sophie. I do surgery and stuff." He slides up to the end of the table on a rolling stool. "You're going to feel my hand on the inside of your thigh."

He adjusts the light attached to the end of the table and flips it on. Jesus, there's a light? The fluorescent lights in this room aren't enough?

"Relax. I'm just checking externally first." I feel his fingers on me, his touch gentle.

How many times have I imagined his head in a similar position? This is so awkward. *Focus on this sterile room, Soph. Do not embarrass yourself.*

"So you just like college students or something? So you volunteer?" Oh, shit. I think I just accused him of being some kind of creep.

I feel him pause. On my vagina. Because he's touching my vagina as I accuse him of being into examining college girls. Help me.

"My family donated this clinic years ago, long before your college days, Miss Tisdale. My great-grandfather was a physician and he believed in giving back, donating his time to help when he could. I donate a few hours a week in his honor."

I hear Luke pick up the plastic-wrapped item off the tray and pry the plastic open. It reminds me of the sound when they open the sterilized instrument pack while I'm getting a pedicure. Great. Now I'll probably get turned on getting a pedicure. As if I need another fetish. I think being attracted to your gynecologist is enough fetish to last a lifetime.

"I specialize in infertility and high-risk pregnancies. Patients with financial resources." The wheels of the stool squeak across the linoleum floor. "The flip side of women desperate to have a child are women desperate not to. One of the goals of this clinic is to provide students with easy access to contraception and preventative care, so their futures are not derailed by a baby they didn't plan for. That's something I can easily help out with by volunteering a couple hours a week."

Oh.

"We keep the gel room temperature so it's not too cold," Luke explains as he coats the speculum. I stare at it as his hand glides over the instrument, back and forth. I feel his fingers on me again, spreading me open. He places the tip at my entrance. "You're going to feel some pressure. I'm using the small speculum so it shouldn't be too uncomfortable." He slowly slides the instrument inside of me.

Fuck, that is tight. My toes curl in the stirrups and I arch my back a little.

"Relax." Luke's hand is on my thigh again, his thumb rubbing reassuringly back and forth. "I need to dilate this enough to check your cervix and get a swab, okay?"

I feel a slight spreading sensation and a click. The light is re-angled again as he grabs something from the table.

"Quick swab and you're done. Your cervix looks great."

My cervix looks great. Is that a gynecologist pickup line? I laugh internally.

"All done." I hear the release on the device as he dials it closed. "Relax for me, Sophie. I need to slide the speculum out. It's easier on you if you relax." I can feel the fingers of one hand spreading me open as he slowly slides the instrument out.

He stands up and squirts a clear jelly onto the tip of his blue-gloved right index finger. "I'm going to press down on your abdomen from the outside while I insert a finger to check your internal organs."

Holy fuck. He's sliding a finger inside of me. It feels good. Smaller than the speculum. His other hand slips under the paper gown. I tighten around his finger and suppress making any sound.

"Please relax," Luke says, like he's trying to be reassuring, but I suspect he's exasperated with me. His finger slides in and out a fraction as he pushes from above and I know I'm wet enough that he didn't need whatever gel he squirted onto his gloves. He moves his hand around my abdomen, pressing down as his finger moves inside of me. I really like how that feels, the pressure from above with his finger inside of me. I clench on his finger involuntarily and feel a small spasm ripple through me. Oh my god. I think I just had an orgasm. Holy shit. Did he notice? It was small. Maybe he didn't notice.

Luke clears his throat, slides his finger out of me and covers me with the paper gown, not making eye contact. He *so* noticed. Stepping back, he tosses the blue gloves into the trash on his way to the sink. "You can sit up now, Sophie."

I remove my feet from the stirrups and sit up, immediately missing the ceiling poster because now I'm not sure what to focus on. I end up staring at a poster on STD's.

"I'll give you a minute to get dressed and then I'll meet you up front with a prescription for you."

Marie drops the magazine into a holder by the door as Luke exits the room. "Let me move these for you, hun." She folds the stirrups back into the table. "See, that was easy, right?" She pats my knee and turns to the door. "Just come to the checkout desk when you're ready."

I sigh as the door closes. What the hell. I'm going to have to quit my job at Grind Me. Or hide in the back room every time Luke comes in. Dr. Miller, not Luke. This might be a new low in my life.

I get up, tearing the stupid paper cover in the process. There's a wet spot on the paper. Is that normal? Am I supposed to clean up after myself? Why does no one prepare you for this before going to the gynecologist? I toss the paper gown over the wet spot and grab a paper towel to wipe myself with. I make quick work of getting redressed before checking my reflection in the mirror. I look a little flushed. I just went farther with Luke than I did with Scott in two years of dating. "You're a pervert," I say to my reflection before sitting down to pull on my shoes.

Wait. Which socks am I wearing today? I pause, shoe in hand. The ones with the pink stripes around the top. I flip my foot. Classy. That's what's written on the bottom of my left foot. And on the bottom of my right foot? Bitch. I'm wearing my classy bitch socks. That I just flashed at Luke while my legs were spread. Can this appointment get any worse?

I open the exam room door and walk to the checkout desk. It's a counter really. Just inside the exit. Luke is standing there, writing on a chart as I approach. He sets down the pen and checks his watch. It's big and expensive-looking and looks perfect on his wrist. What is it about a watch on a man? It's so hot. Most guys my age just whip cell phones out of their pocket to check the time. Maybe they'd wear watches if they really understood the appeal to women.

Luke sees me approaching now and slides a paper bag off the counter. "Here's a three-month supply of birth control. The clinic will refill your prescription for free as long as you're a student. Do not let it lapse because you can't make it to the clinic to pick up a refill. You can refill with one month remaining, so that gives you a month before you run out. Understand?"

His tone is firm and I'm somewhat offended. I'm not stupid. "Yes, I understand, Dr. Miller."

He continues on about the dangers of antibiotics decreasing the effectiveness and using backup birth control while on antibiotics and for a week afterward. Really, it's stuff I learned either in sixth-grade health or from watching Lifetime movies, but I listen.

"You can start the pill today. You'll need to use backup birth control for a week. You should still use condoms unless your partner has been tested. There's a supply in the bag and you can always get more from the clinic. Any questions?"

"I thought you were a lawyer."

He just stares at me for a second. I think we're both surprised I just said that.

"And I thought you were... not a student." His gaze lingers on mine for a second. I could never get tired of looking at those eyes, not that I'll have the opportunity to see them again.

"Take care, Sophie. Good luck." He pats my arm and walks away.

Did he just wish me good luck with getting laid? I stuff the paper bag into my backpack and exit the clinic. I look back over the entrance. Rutherford Miller Memorial Health Center is engraved into the stone above the door, underneath big black metal letters affixed to the building spelling out Student Clinic.

Four

I pass the campus shuttle stop outside the clinic in favor of walking. It's warmed up a little now that the sun is out and I don't feel like being cooped up on a bus right now.

There are walking paths all over campus. I can make it from the clinic back to my dorm on foot. Or maybe I'll just head to my next class early. I don't feel like facing my roommate right now either.

My cheeks burn as I recall the last half hour. Is there something wrong with me? Do I have some kind of doctor fetish? To be fair, I was attracted to Luke before I knew he was a doctor, let alone my doctor. But seeing him in that lab coat should have squashed it. It didn't, it made it worse.

The position of authority was a huge turn-on. Would it have been if I hadn't already been fantasizing about him for weeks? I don't think so.

How can I be this attracted to a man I barely know? It was insta-lust for me the first day I saw him. I'm not this attracted to Mike and he's my boyfriend. I'm a bad person. Who feels that way about their own boyfriend? Or am I attracted to Luke because he's unattainable?

Did I date a guy platonically for two years because it was safe? I'm not a risk-taker. I'm good. I never wanted to be my mother. I never wanted to derail my life with an unplanned pregnancy and burden my grandparents with another infant they didn't plan for.

I know my grandfather worked longer than he would have if they hadn't had to raise me. And they've put off retiring to Florida for too long, wanting to be nearby while I went to college. I finally convinced them to list the house once I entered my senior year at the university a few weeks ago.

I haven't lived at home for more than a few weeks during the summer since high school, but they never wanted me to feel like I had no place to go back to. I had to promise them that if I didn't find a job after college that afforded a decent apartment, I'd come to Florida and stay with them. And they refuse to look at anything in Florida that doesn't have room for me, even if I only stay there a few nights a year.

I make it to the Hymer building early for my next class. I'm debating whether I want to wait inside or out when Everly exits the building. We don't usually cross paths at Hymer on Tuesdays, but I am early.

"Hey, bitch, did you get laid at the doctor's office? You look different."

I roll my eyes at Everly.

"What?"

"Lukesagynecologist."

"What?" Everly tilts her head like I'm talking crazy.

"Luke is a gynecologist. At the student health clinic."

"Shut the fuck up." I think I've managed to shock Everly. "I did not see this coming." She looks at me. "So?"

"So?" I ask.

"So you rescheduled the appointment with another doctor?"

"No. I kept the appointment."

"You kinky bitch, you did not! Stop it."

"I did. I was already sitting on the exam table wearing a paper gown when he walked in. What was I supposed to do?"

"Was it good for you?" She grins at me suggestively.

"Everly!"

"Bitch, I know you enjoyed it. At least a little."

"You think there's something wrong with me, don't you?"

"Sophie, no. That guy has no business being a gynecologist. It's not fair to women."

"I think he's technically an obstetrician."

"Same difference."

"The nurse said he runs a department at the hospital."

"Well done, Sophie. When you crush, you crush classy."

"Ugh." I cringe. "That reminds me. Do you keep your socks on during a gynecologist exam?"

"Off. So, did you get your prescription?"

"Yeah." I nod. "And a bag full of condoms." I pat my backpack.

"Aww. Dr. Luke cares about your safety."

"You understand I am never waiting on him again, right?"

"Oh, yeah. I figured that out about thirty seconds into this conversation."

"What are you doing on this side of campus anyway? You don't have a class in the Hymer building, do you?"

Everly snorts. "Extra credit."

I groan. "I'm not even gonna ask."

She adjusts her backpack over her shoulder and grins at me. "Your virgin ears couldn't handle it anyway. I gotta run, Sophie. I can't miss my next class. See you on Thursday!"

"Wait, why will you see me on Thursday?" I ask, confused.

"Your waxing appointment!" she calls out as she walks away. "I decided to escort you there myself. Otherwise you won't go."

I'm walking backwards towards the building as Everly shouts directions to meet her in the lobby of my dorm on Thursday when I collide with a muscular wall.

"Oomph."

"Oh, I'm sorry! I wasn't—" I turn around and see Mike grinning at me. "Oh, it's you." I laugh, relieved.

Mike wraps his arms around me and nuzzles my neck. "What's this about a waxing appointment?" he murmurs into my ear.

I guess my vagina is an open topic today. *Viva la vagina.*

Mike stands several inches taller than me, but not so tall that I can't press up on my toes and kiss him, which I do now, looping my arms around his neck. His sandy brown hair is messy and needs a cut. "Can you get your room to yourself on Saturday night?"

His eyes light up. "Yeah?"

"Yes," I state firmly.

He slides his hands into the back pockets of my jeans. "I can get my room to ourselves right now."

I laugh and slip out of his arms. "Saturday," I say. "I've got to get to class. Besides, I still need to get that wax you're so nosy about." I smile and start backing towards the building.

His eyes drop to my crotch and he sighs. "We could do a before and after?" he calls out, but I'm already on the steps.

"Saturday!" I reply and walk into the building.

Five

I bury my head under the blankets as my roommate's phone alarm beeps. Wednesdays are my sleep-in day and Jean's early class day. Figures.

I hear Jean grab her shower stuff and exit the room. I never saw her yesterday. She must have slipped back into the room after I fell asleep last night. I haven't seen her since... urgh. Monday afternoon.

I walked in on her and her boyfriend having sex. Not a post-coital cuddle. I'm in college, I've walked in on that plenty. And not a demure romp under the covers. Nope. Hell, I had a roommate freshman year who'd do that with me asleep in the next bed. I learned to pee before I went to bed if I didn't want to wake up to something awkward that year.

No, I walked in on Jeannie and Jonathan midday. Lights on. Mid-thrust. In profile to the door. And she was getting double-penetrated. By Jonathan and a toy.

It was like walking into a TMI brick wall. Too much information.

I throw the covers off my head and stare at the ceiling. I mean, I'm curious. But I prefer to be educated by online porn, not my roommate live and in person.

The door clicks open and Jean slips in and takes care

to shut the door quietly behind her. She's dried her long hair and dressed in the bathroom in an effort to let me sleep in.

"I'm awake."

"Oh. Sorry, Soph." She looks contrite as she stuffs her shower basket into her bookshelf. Our tiny room is crammed with all the necessities of dorm life.

She looks at me and pauses.

We both burst into laughter.

"I was hoping I'd stayed away long enough for you to forget." She collapses onto the bed and wipes away tears of laughter. "I thought you were in class. I am so sorry you walked in on us."

"Professor LaRoche let us leave early after a group project."

"No, it's not your fault. I should have texted you." She gets off the bed and digs through her dresser drawer. "Thank you for not judging me."

"Oh, I'm judging you," I reply. "I'm awarding you a perfect ten. On flexibility." I can't even finish the sentence before I start laughing again.

"Oh my God. I have never been so happy to have a class I have to be at." She swipes some lip gloss on and screws the container shut.

"Wait!" I call out. "Before I forget to tell you. I'm spending the night at Mike's on Saturday. You've got the place to yourself." I spread my arms wide to indicate our tiny dorm room.

"Okay, good to know." She pauses with her hand on the doorknob, slinging her backpack over one shoulder. "See you later, Sophie."

I flop back onto my pillow and stare at the closed

door. I have econ studying to do. I hear doors opening and closing up and down the hallway. A cell phone is ringing somewhere.

Jeannie won't be back for at least two hours. I reach over and slip my iPad off my desk. In a room this small, I don't even have to get out of bed to reach.

I flip open the cover and the device springs to life. I tap on the internet browser and navigate to my favorite porn site, Porn Hole.

Propping open the iPad on the case stand, I navigate through the available videos, looking for something promising. Here's one. Play.

I slip a hand into my pajama bottoms and touch myself. I rub my clit with the tips of two fingers. The blood rushes to my clit as I play with myself. Wait. This girl's voice is so annoying. I'm only two minutes into this video and already my ears hurt. I wonder if this guy is wearing ear plugs. Mute.

I forward to the penetration. That's what I like. I watch as the man on screen slides into the woman. By the contorted look on her face I'm glad I muted her already. The camera zooms in on where they're joined. I watch him slide in and out. He's average-sized, based on my limited porn-viewing research. Maybe a little bigger than Scott.

I rub my clit vigorously in rhythm to the couple on screen. That looks like it feels good. The in and out, her body stretching to accommodate his. I wonder how big Mike is. I haven't sucked him off. After two years of giving Scott blow jobs with no return favors, I'm not exactly in a rush.

I bet Luke is bigger than this guy on screen. He looks

like he'd be substantial. I wonder what Luke would feel like inside of me? His finger felt snug.

I rub harder and use my other hand to pinch my breast. I imagine that it's his fingers touching me. It felt nice when he touched me on the exam table, but it was clinical. I squeeze my breast, imagining it's Luke grabbing me roughly. His hands are so much bigger than mine. Stronger.

There was a moment on the exam table when his finger was inside of me, and his thumb swiped across my clit. I clench at the memory.

He's a big guy. Solid. Muscular. More filled out than a college guy. What would it feel like to have him inside of me? It wouldn't be comfortable at first. I know that. But after, after he stroked back and forth, easing into my body. After he sank himself inside of me all the way, my body stretching to accommodate him. After I adjusted to the invasion and he started to really move. What would that feel like with Luke?

Would he bend me over and use my hips to anchor himself as he thrust in and out? Or would he lay me on my back and part my thighs? Settle between them, resting his upper body on his forearms and sucking at my tits as he thrust?

I come.

Thinking about Luke.

Not my boyfriend, Mike.

Did I think about Mike once? I try to recall. Disgusted with myself, I grab my shower supplies and head to the communal bathroom at the end of the hall.

* * *

I hang my damp towel on my closet door and slip into a pair of old faded jeans before pulling a long-sleeved powder-blue tee shirt over my head. Pulling my still-damp hair over one shoulder, I braid the end of it and secure it with an elastic, then shove my feet into an old pair of Ugg boots, sans socks. I've had these things for years, a Christmas present from my grandparents back in high school.

Grabbing a textbook, I take a seat at my desk and crack it open. This is so dull. I'm tapping my pen against the desk when my phone chirps, like I've missed a call. I pick it up, seeing I've missed three calls, all from my grandmother's cell phone number.

My heart races a little. Why would she call me three times in a row? It looks like I missed all three calls while I was in the shower. I hit play. The first message is a hang up, followed by a message from my grandmother asking me to call her. The third is my grandmother again. "Sophie, it's Gram. Your grandfather slipped on a ladder cleaning the gutters. I'm sure everything will be fine, but we're at Baldwin Memorial getting him checked out." She sounds a little distressed. "I'm sure it's fine." The message ends.

Oh, no. I check the call log. She called forty minutes ago. I hit the call back button and pace to the window. Answer, answer, answer. Please answer.

"Hello?"

"Grandma!" I'm so relieved to be speaking with her and not her voicemail.

"Oh, Sophie, good. You got my messages."

"What happened? Is Grandpa okay? What happened?"

I'm firing off questions without giving her time to answer.

"He insisted on cleaning out those damn gutters himself and slipped off the ladder. He hit his head and blacked out for a minute. The hospital is going to scan to make sure his back and neck are okay."

"What did the doctor say?"

"Oh, honey, I don't know. We got here a couple of hours ago. We're still in the ER."

"I'm on my way," I say, grabbing my wristlet with my ID, keycard and some cash. Jacket. Where's my jacket? I grab a University of Pennsylvania hoodie.

"Are you sure, Sophie? You don't have a class?"

"No, I don't have any classes this afternoon, Gram. I'll be there soon."

Six

I walk into the front entrance at Baldwin Memorial Hospital, grateful I found someone at my dorm with a car willing to drop me off. My grandmother called while I was en route and said they'd taken Grandpa to radiology and she'd be waiting in the ER. I check in at the visitor desk and am given directions to the ER and find my grandmother sitting in a little curtained-off room flipping through a magazine.

"Sophie, honey, thank you for coming." Gram hugs me.

"Of course. Are you okay?"

"I'm fine, I was on the ground where I belong. Your grandfather, on the other hand, may have a concussion."

"Grandma! A concussion is serious."

"Well, we're in the right place to have it checked out. How is school?" She pats the empty chair next to her and I obligingly sit and update her on all the happenings at school.

My grandfather is eventually wheeled back into the room with word that they'll be back with the results "soon." Then we wait. And wait some more. I give Grandpa all the same updates I gave Grandma between nurses bustling in and out and the never-ending waiting.

Grandma finally agrees that she would like a coffee after I've asked her several times. I think she just wants something to break up the waiting at this point.

* * *

I head back to the main entrance in search of a hospital cafeteria. I'm standing lost in the lobby looking for a helpful sign with an arrow to point me in the right direction when I feel a hand on my arm.

"Sophie. What are you doing here? Is everything okay?"

It's Luke. His hand is still cupping my elbow and his eyes are concerned.

"Yeah," I say, but I shake my head. "I'm fine. It's my grandpa. He fell off a ladder. We're just waiting for some test results. I'm getting my grandmother a coffee, if I can find the cafeteria." I'm babbling. Luke has dropped my elbow and put his hands in his expensive suit pockets. "Why are you here?" I ask, confused.

He smiles at me. "Hospital. Doctor. I hang out here a lot."

"Oh. This is your hospital? But you're in a suit. Why are you never in scrubs?"

"I'm not usually in scrubs unless I've got surgery. And I don't schedule surgeries for Wednesdays, because the board meets on Wednesdays." He tugs on the end of my braid. "Would you prefer I wear scrubs when getting coffee, Sophie?"

"I, um. No. The suits are fine." I'm flustered.

"Come on, I'll walk you to the hospital coffee shop. It's got a better selection than the cafeteria." His hand on my back maneuvers me to a hallway off the lobby. The coffee shop is just around the corner. I must have been too distracted to notice it earlier. "Is your grandfather okay?"

"I don't know. I think so? He had a CAT scan a couple of hours ago and we've been sitting in the ER waiting on results."

Luke nods. "Okay."

I'm twisting my phone around and around in my hands. "Thanks for helping me find the coffee shop," I offer when he continues to stand there looking at me.

"Are your parents here Sophie?"

I look away. "No. I don't have—" I look at him. "No, it's just me and my grandparents."

He places a hand on my wrist, stilling me from spinning my phone yet again. "It's going to be fine, Sophie."

"Right." I offer a weak smile. "Thanks." I get in line to get my grandmother the coffee she doesn't really want, and watch Luke walk away.

* * *

I'm back in the ER with the coffee for just a few minutes before a doctor enters the curtained room.

"Sorry to have kept you waiting. I'm Dr. McElroy and I have the results from the CAT scan. They look good but I still want to keep you overnight for observation. You have a slight concussion and I want to keep an eye on that." She smiles at each of us like concussion-watching is her favorite pastime. "We're going to get you moved up to a room in just a minute. And Mrs. Tisdale, you're welcome to stay the night in Mr. Tisdale's room if you like. The couches open to very comfortable beds if you want to be nearby."

The doctor excuses herself as my phone beeps.

Your grandfather is being moved to a
room for the night for observation.
Dr. McElroy is an expert in her field & is
only admitting him as a precaution. Let me
know if you need anything. Luke

I stare at my phone, dumbfounded. This is nice? Creepy? I look up. I feel like I'm being watched. How does he know so much? More importantly, how did he get my phone number?

Dr. McElroy breezes back into the curtained room with an orderly and announces they're ready to move us. I look at her with more interest than before. She's in standard-issue scrubs and a doctor's lab coat, but I can't help but notice how beautiful she is. Huge blue eyes framed by dark lashes so thick I wonder if they're fake. They look real. Her dark glossy hair is cut in a stylish bob. There's not a stray hair out of place.

I find myself wondering if this is the kind of woman Luke goes for. Accomplished. Polished, even in scrubs. My curiosity questions if they've slept together. They work in the same hospital. The staff are always sleeping together, at least on the medical dramas I watch on TV. They could be sleeping together currently for all I know. The thought causes a wave of discomfort to flash through me.

We sat waiting for hours. Then I bumped into Luke

and within minutes Dr. McElroy was at our side. Is Luke doing a favor for me? Or is Dr. McElroy doing a favor for Luke?

The orderly is a tiny girl who introduces herself as Kaylee. She doesn't look big enough to maneuver an occupied hospital bed through the halls, but she unlocks the bed wheels with a confident flip of her foot and weaves us out of the ER with an ease that belies her size.

I express my admiration at her strength and she laughs. "I'm a mom," she tells me. "A grown man in a rolling bed is easier than toddlers in a double stroller, trust me."

I laugh and drop back as she works the bed around a tight corner and onto an elevator. She pushes the button for five and chats with my grandmother while I check my phone again. I should reply. Right?

Thank you.

You're welcome, Sophie.

How did you get my number?

Hospital database. You're listed as an emergency contact on your grandfather's file.

That seems like a misuse of the hospital database. And a violation of HIPPO laws.

HIPPO!

Damn autocorrect! HIPPA.

I think your admonishment lost its luster at the word hippo.

Yeah. A little.

Can you keep a secret, Sophie?

>In general, or yours?

Mine.

>Sure.

Then it's our secret.

I bite my lip to suppress a smile as I slip the phone into my pocket. Kaylee expertly guides us through the doorway of room 5853 and locks the bed wheels into place before wishing Grandpa a speedy recovery. I stay and get them settled in. More for me than them. I need to know they're okay before I leave.

They tell me they got a good offer on the house and that they've found a couple of places in Islamorada, Florida. It's a village of islands located in the Florida Keys, they tell me. Average highs of eighty-nine degrees, sunny days and clear water for snorkeling. My grandparents are only in their sixties. They're active and in great shape, they'd love a climate that allowed more time outdoors.

I encourage them to take the offer and go. Don't spend another winter in Pennsylvania when Florida is just a short plane ride away. I think they're finally accepting that I am graduating in the spring and I won't be coming back to live with them.

I text Mike and ask if he can pick me up and drive me back to campus. He agrees, so I give my grandparents one last hug and head to the lobby to wait.

Exiting the elevator when it reaches the lobby, I find it's busier than earlier. I take two steps before I spot Luke.

He's standing, hands in pockets, staring right at me. He's talking to another doctor in a white lab coat with a stethoscope draped around his neck.

I falter a moment. Is he waiting for me? Why? I decide I'm not going to interrupt him and keep walking, intending to find a bench out front where I can sit while I wait for Mike to pick me up.

I exit the hospital and I'm hit with a blast of cold air. Maybe I'll wait inside instead. I turn around and head back in, finding Luke's eyes still on me. It's weird. There's nowhere to sit where I can still see the cars pulling up, so I stand in front of the glass windows instead.

"I talked to the lead tech in radiology and Dr. McElroy. His back and neck are fine. They'll just keep him for observation on the concussion."

Luke is right beside me. I have to look up a little to see his face. I'm not usually standing right next to him. He's taller than I thought.

"Thank you. Whoever you talked to, it worked. We finally saw a doctor and he got moved right away." I untie my hoodie from around my waist and slip my arms inside the sleeves.

Luke shrugs, his gaze roaming over my face. "How'd the condoms work out?"

What? I'm stunned. He can't ask me that. I look at him, but he's not backing down in the slightest. He's staring at me like he expects I'll answer him.

"I haven't used them yet." I'm not sure why I'm answering this man. His question is so out of line. Yet I feel compelled to respond to him.

"Are you going to?"

What exactly is he asking me? If I'm planning on

41

having sex? Or if I'm planning on being safe when I have sex?

"Yes."

He's silent now. His jaw ticks.

"You've waited a long time."

"I have." Where is he going with this?

"Is he worth it?" Luke's eyes are dark, yet his expression is curious.

Oh. That's where he's going with this conversation. Some kind of parental 'does he respect you' second-guessing. I'm twenty-one. I don't need this from him.

"Maybe it's not about him. Maybe it's about me." I'm angry now. Who is he to question me about any of this? And why am I answering him? Because of my misplaced lust?

A car honks outside and my attention is diverted from Luke's face. Mike is outside, idling in the no-parking lane, trying to get my attention.

"Is that him?" Luke is standing even closer than he was before.

"Yes."

"Sophie—"

I cut him off. I've had enough of this. "Thanks, Dr. Miller, for everything. I'll use the condoms, I promise. I'll even YouTube directions so I don't screw it up, okay? So don't worry about me. I've got it covered." I laugh. "Literally, I'll make sure it's covered, okay?"

He looks surprised. Does no one call him on his bullshit?

"My ride is here." I shake my head. "My boyfriend is here." I correct myself. "Thank you for your help with my grandfather and your repeated safe-sex talks. I promise you I will not show up at the clinic knocked up."

"Sophie." Now Luke sounds pissed. What the hell is he pissed about? I don't care for his tone. Who is this man to me? No one. Mike is outside waiting for me. Mike who never gives me mixed signals. Mike who makes it clear he wants me. Mike who is not an inappropriate match.

"Thanks, Dr. Miller. Goodbye." I walk away.

Seven

"Let's go!" Everly sings out as the door swings shut behind her. She's grinning at me as if we have exciting plans. She's just walked into my dorm room unannounced, coat on, black hair pulled into a low pony tail. She's ready to go.

I'm lying across my bed cuddling a textbook for my business ethics class. I'm ready to go nowhere.

"Where are we going?" I ask. I'm pretty sure I know, but I am the queen of denial.

Incidentally, my ex-boyfriend Scott is now very happily dating. A personal trainer, named James. I saw them once on 34th Street, holding hands and laughing about some shared joke. They'd looked happy and I'd felt a wave of jealousy. Not over Scott. I'd always known on some level that we were just coasting together—Scott until he came out of the closet and me until I felt willing to take the next step. Because that step? It's a risk.

My mom got pregnant at sixteen. I have no idea how careful she was or wasn't. From what I remember of her she wasn't careful about anything. All I know is that I never want to be her. I never want to repay my grandparents for taking me in and raising me by repeating that cycle. And I never want to put myself in a position

45

where I'd have to choose between abortion, adoption or asking for help.

Sex was one big risk. Is that paranoid? To avoid sex on the small chance that the pill would fail and I'd end up pregnant? Maybe. But my early years left a big impact on me. I'm not going there, so Luke can shove his safe-sex speeches up his ass. I'm the last girl who needs to hear it.

So when I saw Scott and his boyfriend on the street that day I felt a little wistful over what they had together. Who doesn't want that?

Mike has been flirting with me since junior year. I ignored him, mostly. It wasn't that serious. He was always with one girl or another. When we started classes this fall we ended up in Business Ethics together and this time when he flirted, I encouraged it.

"You know where we're going, Sophie. Your pubes are not going to wax themselves," Everly says, interrupting my thoughts.

"Please never say the word pubes again."

Everly grabs a hoodie off the back of my chair and tosses it at me. "Let's go. We have appointments."

"How'd you get in the building anyway?" I ask as I pull on my old Uggs and grab my bag.

"I bumped into Jeannie out front, she buzzed me in."

Exiting the front door of Jacobsen, we take the sidewalk towards the nearest university bus stop. It's a beautiful afternoon in Philadelphia. The air has that crisp fresh smell that only comes with fall.

I pull the sweatshirt over my head as we walk, stuffing my cell phone into the front pocket. "Anything I need to know before this appointment?" I ask, glancing at Everly as we walk.

"No. Stop being a pussy. You're gonna get naked with Leah. She's gonna apply wax to your lady bits and then rip the hair out by the root until you're as smooth as a baby's ass."

"Huh. It's strange how apprehensive I am about this based on your vivid description." I swerve to avoid a cyclist. "I mean, it sounds great. It must just be me."

"Clearly it's just you," Everly responds as we board the student bus. We can take this to the edge of campus and then walk down Sansom Street.

"What are you doing this weekend?" I ask Everly as she frowns at her cell phone.

"Going home," she replies, thumbs flying over the touch screen of her phone, tapping out a text. "My brother is getting married."

"Oh! That sounds fun." I think it would have been fun to grow up with siblings. Everly's brother is quite a bit older than her, but still, a big brother would have been nice. "Are you taking the train?" I know Everly grew up somewhere outside of New York City. The train between Philadelphia and New York is a common way to travel.

"I better not be taking the train," she replies with a final tap to her phone. She smiles.

I'm confused by her response. "Is someone driving down to pick you up?"

"No." She crosses her legs and rests the phone on her thigh. "Professor Camden is driving me home."

I'm never sure how seriously to take this crush she has on Professor Camden. Though lately it's bordering on an obsession. She's mentioned him on and off for years, but she's never lacked a boyfriend. Plus he's a professor.

"Really?" I ask. "Professor Camden is driving you to

New York?" I know I sound dubious. Professor Camden is really good-looking and ten years older than us. At least. Not to mention a professor. So completely off limits.

I'm not judging. My crush on Luke turned out to be even more inappropriate than I'd imagined. I just don't want Everly to get hurt. Everly tends to get what she wants, but I'm afraid this time she wants something she just can't have.

Everly opens her mouth to respond when her phone rings. She glances at the screen and smirks before giving me a huge smile. "Yes, he is." She presses the green answer button and brings the phone to her ear. In a sweet voice I'm not familiar with she answers, "Yes, Professor Camden?"

She pauses, I assume listening.

"So now you want me to stop with the professor title, Finn?" Her voice is steady, but her foot bounces as she talks. "I'll be ready at eight." Her foot is still now, and she's picking at a loose thread in a hole in her jeans. "I live in Stroh, Finn. I'll be waiting out front at eight. Bye." She pushes the red end call button on her phone and sighs.

I glance at her, a thousand questions written on my face.

"Finn Camden is my brother's best friend. He's also the best man in his wedding this weekend. I'm a bridesmaid." She shoves the cell into her pocket. "He didn't want to drive me to New York, so I texted my brother and told him I was going to have to take the train alone late tonight." She shrugs and offers a little pout. "Because I knew he'd tell Finn to drive me and Finn can't tell my brother that he doesn't want to be stuck in a car alone with me. Due to my"—she pauses and does the air quote sign with her fingers—"inappropriate advances."

"Wow." There's so much to respond to in that statement I'm not sure where to begin.

"Right? He's being ridiculous. I don't have that much time left."

"Time?" I question.

"Yeah. We're graduating in seven months. I don't have any reason to stay in Philly after that. This is the optimal time window in which to make him fall in love with me."

"Um."

"He's finally single," she continues on. "I need him to accept us before he finds someone else and before I graduate."

"Accept you?"

"That last girlfriend, just no." She shakes her head. "He has no idea how much he's going to appreciate me in comparison. I guess I should thank her for that. But I won't."

I'm not sure how to respond to that, but the conversation ends as we've reached our stop. We step out onto Sansom with Everly leading the way.

"This place looks sketchy," I say as we climb the stairs of doom.

"Relax. I would not let you get a sketchy Brazilian wax." Everly pulls open the door. "Have a little faith, bitch."

Everly checks us in as I take a seat to wait. A minute later a pretty girl comes out from a back room and hugs Everly. She glances over at me and smiles. "Hi! I'm

Leah." Wait. This is our waxer? She looks like she's only a few years older than we are. I was imagining a nice older woman I'd never bump into again.

"So which one of you wants to go first?" Leah looks between us. This girl has the most perfect eyebrows I've ever seen. I wonder if she waxes them herself.

"She'll go first," we both say at the same time.

"Oh, no, you're going first. Before you chicken out."

"Fine," I grumble in reply. I get off the couch and so does Everly.

"What are you doing?" I ask her.

"I'm coming with."

"Uh, no. That cannot be normal. I draw the line at having you watch."

"Yeah, that is not okay. You can't come with if Sophie doesn't want you to," Leah states firmly. I'm surprised. She's got a hippie-chick vibe and a nose ring. I thought she'd invite Everly back with open arms.

Yes! "Yeah, Everly, that is not okay." I smile smugly and wave on my way into the back room.

Eight

"Take off your pants and lie on your back." Leah is stirring a pot of wax on a counter set up along the wall.

I falter for a moment. Just take off my pants? I pictured her leaving the room and me getting at least a paper gown to cover myself with. Everly was wrong. The gynecologist visit was less awkward than this.

Leah turns her head and sees me just standing there. "Your underwear too. We're doing a full Brazilian, right?"

Okay then. I nod and toe my shoes off without bending over. I unzip and slide my jeans off before folding them and placing them on an empty chair with my bag. So, my underwear. This is weird. I slip them off too and look at my folded jeans. I should tuck my underwear under my jeans, right? I know I'm standing here naked but I don't want her to see my underwear just lying on the chair.

I glance down. Socks. Dammit with the socks again. On or off? On. Definitely on. She's not waxing my feet. I hop onto the table and lie back. No poster on the ceiling here. I stuff my hands into the pocket of my hoodie. It's so weird that I'm only naked from the waist down.

Leah turns away from the pot of wax and inspects me. Literally. "Okay, let's see what we have to work with here.

Pull your knees up and drop them to the side. Like a frog."

"There's no poster on the ceiling!" I blurt out.

"What?" Leah looks confused.

"Um. You should have a poster. On the ceiling. For me to look at. Or maybe a TV?" I look at Leah. She's not looking at me anymore though. She's got a big popsicle stick of wax in her hand and she's about to slather it on my body.

This is it. I'm about to die. Of humiliation. My hand bumps the cell still stuffed in my hoodie pocket. I should send a goodbye message. I pull out my phone. I text Everly and tell her I hate her.

The first coat of wax hits my skin. That's not so bad. It's warm. Kinda pleasant even. Minus the fact that I'm lying half naked on a table in front of a woman I just met.

Leah drops the stick in the trash and presses a cloth on top of the wax. Pressing it down with her hand. Yeah. This is fantastic.

Not.

Leah presses one hand flat against my abdomen and rips the wax strip off with the other.

I wait for a blinding pain combined with a flash of white light inviting me to cross over to the other side. Ouch. That hurt. But I don't think it's going to kill me. It wasn't so bad. It burns a little.

It's more embarrassing than anything. I let out a huge breath I didn't realize I was holding.

Leah's back with another stick full of wax. Spreading and ripping. "Looks good!" she chirps from between my thighs. "Your boyfriend is going to love this!"

"Yeah," I reply. "I'm sure he will. So, do you wax

yourself?"

"Oh, no," Leah replies. "We wax each other."

"What?"

"The other waxers. We just grab whoever's not busy and do each other."

"You let your co-workers wax your vagina? People you see every day? And meet after work for drinks?"

Leah laughs. "Yeah. Who cares?" She shrugs. "You have to be careful with co-workers though. Sometimes we mess with each other for a laugh."

"Practical jokes with wax?" I ask.

"Exactly. One time"—she has to stop because she's laughing—"one time Laura waxed Katie's bush into the shape of a goldfish cracker." I try to discreetly check out my vagina in case Everly's arranged for some practical joke to my nether regions. "Katie was into some 80's phase where she was only doing her bikini line." Leah has regained her composure. "Totally unacceptable, obviously."

"Obviously." I don't agree, but I'm half naked on a table and Leah is controlling the destiny of my vaginal hair, so I nod.

"I mean, get some leg warmers if you're going retro. Am I right?" Thankfully Leah doesn't wait for me to respond to that before continuing. "So Katie doesn't even notice. Until that night when her husband goes down on her and starts laughing so hard they have to stop." Leah tries not to laugh, which causes a snort to escape.

"So what did she do?" I ask. "Fix it herself? Or live with it?"

"Oh, no." Leah is suddenly very serious. "That is not

okay, Sophie. Never wax your own vagina." She shakes her head. "Never. Waxing yourself is the devil. The pain is totally different when you're inflicting it on yourself." She waves at my vagina. "This isn't so bad, right?"

"No." I have to agree. "It's not that bad. I thought it would hurt worse."

Leah nods and rips another strip of hair off my body, then scrutinizes her work. "There's a few strays. Hold on." She returns and leans over my crotch with a pair of tweezers and yanks.

Oh. My. God. Why does it hurt so much more one hair at a time? I can't believe this woman is hovering over my vagina with a pair of tweezers. I want to tell her not to bother, Mike can deal with a few stray hairs, but I feel like it would be rude to tell her how to do her job. On my vagina.

My phone beeps. It's a picture of a kitten. In a bikini. *Don't be a pussy, wax your kitty,* Everly's typed.

"Almost done!" Leah says. "Knees up to the ceiling now and hold 'em."

Did she just ask me to flash my asshole at her? "What?" I ask.

"We need to get the hair between the cheeks now." Leah picks my leg up for me and bends it so my knee is at a ninety-degree angle. "Here, put your hand under your knee. Now grab the other one." She turns to grab another wax-covered stick while I put myself into a mental coma to deal with this humiliation.

"Drop your knees open as far as you can." Leah is now spreading wax between my butt cheeks. I wasn't even aware I had hair there. I wonder how much hair I have there? Holy shit, did Luke see my asshole hair? I'm suddenly thankful to Everly. At least Mike won't have to see it.

"We also do vajazzling here! Anything you can think of, we can do." I can't believe Leah is selling me on sparkling my vagina with crystals as she wipes wax between my ass cheeks. "I do a really nice Hello Kitty."

"Um, okay?"

"Your socks." Leah gestures to my feet that are hanging in mid-air. I forgot I'm wearing Hello Kitty socks. I should reconsider my grandparents' offer to live with them in Florida after graduation. I could donate my entire sock collection to Goodwill and wear nothing but flipflops in Florida.

"All done!" Leah tosses the last strip into the trash and grabs a mirror and holds it between my legs. "See? It looks great." She's beaming at me. Does she want me to check out my vagina and compliment her? I take a quick glance in the mirror. Huh, it does look different without hair. "Looks good," I reply politely. I start to get off the table.

"Wait! You need aloe!" Leah pumps a gob of aloe into her hand and smooths it over my vagina. With her hand. My humiliation is complete.

I scoot off the table and dress as quickly as possible while Leah cleans the table and gives me aftercare instructions. She tells me she also does organic goat-milk facials and hands me a coupon for a free facial with my second Brazilian wax. I'm still not sold on this waxing thing, but I'm pretty sure I won't be signing up to get a facial and a Brazilian wax from the same person anytime soon.

Back in the lobby Everly tries to high-five me, but I

just mouth, "I hate you," and flop onto the couch to wait while she goes in for her wax.

Nine

"You're staying all night with Mike, right?" Jean is lying on her bed flipping through a magazine watching me get ready.

"Yes." I turn my attention back to the mirror and finish applying eyeliner to my left eye before coating mascara over my lashes.

"You're sure?" The magazine ruffles as she flips it closed. "You're not coming back for a condom? Or your toothbrush?"

"Nope," I reply. "Both are already in my purse." I scrutinize myself in the mirror. My blue eyes look huge. I've curled my hair into tousled waves falling to the middle of my back. "The room is all yours. You're free to impale yourself on Jonathan's cock in complete privacy."

Jean stops twirling the ends of her blonde hair through her fingers. "Impale myself?" She laughs. "That sounds like a Everly-ism."

I spritz myself with perfume. "Hey! I came up with that one myself, thank you very much."

"What are you guys doing tonight? Besides breaking your hymen."

I hold up two pairs of earrings and Jean points to the dangly ones in my right hand. "We're going for Thai over on Chestnut Street," I reply as I slide the earrings through the tiny holes in my earlobes. "What are you and Jonathan doing?"

"We're just fucking."

"Nice." I sit on the edge of my bed to tug on my black heeled boots. Over black socks. Plain black socks. I had to dig around my drawer to find these, but I'm smug that I've planned accordingly at least once this week. "This is fine for Thai, right?" I ask, indicating my jeans and pink sweater.

Jean waves a dismissive hand at me. "It's perfect. Thai places in University City aren't that fancy." She taps out a text on her cell. "You nervous?"

I cross my legs and lean back on my bed, resting my weight on my hands. "No." I shrug. "I want to get it over with. I waited too long." I grimace. "That sounds awful, doesn't it? Poor Mike."

Jean snorts. "Poor little college boy. Hot virgins sacrificing themselves on his cock."

I laugh as my phone alerts me I have a new message. Glancing at it, I get to my feet. "Mike's downstairs waiting for me. I'll see you tomorrow." I grab a jacket before taking the elevator to the ground floor of my dorm, Jacobsen Hall.

I'm expecting to see Mike waiting for me with one of his big, happy smiles that make the dimples on his cheeks stand out. Instead I find him talking to Paige Gladson. I don't know her very well. She's a fellow business major and I know she lives somewhere in Jacobsen, but I'm not sure which floor. She's wearing loose Juicy Couture sweatpants with Juicy stamped across the ass and a gray tee shirt. No makeup and her blonde hair is bundled on top of her head in a messy knot.

She's pointing a finger in Mike's face as she talks to him. Mike's response is a shrug. He looks bored. My heeled boots click across the tile floor, announcing my arrival. Paige drops her hand and takes a step back.

"Hey, Paige." I smile at her and slip an arm around Mike's waist. He's in dark jeans, a button-front blue plaid shirt and Converse. It's a huge change from his normal classroom attire of jogging pants and Philadelphia Eagles tee shirts. He looks really good and I'm suddenly more enthusiastic about tonight than I was a few minutes ago.

Paige crosses her arms across her chest, but her posture isn't defensive. It's... leery? "Hey, Sophie." She glances at Mike and back to me. "I didn't know you two were together."

"Yeah," I reply, confused. Did Paige once date Mike? He's never lacked female companionship, but I don't recall him with Paige. She doesn't seem jealous, just weird.

"I'll see you next week in Professor Tetrev's class, Paige," Mike tells her. He grabs my hand and tugs me after him towards the door.

His car is parked out front in fifteen-minute parking. He unlocks the car with a remote but stops on the passenger side and pulls open the door for me, slamming it closed after I'm safely tucked inside.

A moment later he's sliding into the driver's seat and starting the engine of the new Camaro. His dad owns a Chevy dealership in suburban Exton and Mike drives a constant stream of new cars.

"What was Paige so animated about? Something in Professor Tetrev's class?"

Mike doesn't take his eyes off the road. "Yeah. You look beautiful, babe." Mike winds our fingers together and brings our joined hands to his lips, kissing the back of mine.

"So do you." I squeeze his hand, Paige forgotten about.

We walk hand in hand down Chestnut after Mike parks in a nearby garage. I'm laughing over something he just said. I really like Mike. I'm happy I'm with him tonight.

University City is bustling with people. It's a gorgeous Saturday night in Philadelphia. The sun has already set and it's cool outside. The darkness and temperature provide a cloak of romance to the evening.

Around us other couples exit and enter restaurants or wait along the curb trying to catch cabs. Car horns honk, the street lamps twinkle in the dark and I love being in the middle of it all.

There's a ten- to fifteen-minute wait for a table when we arrive at the Thai restaurant. They have a bar, so we find an empty hightop table to lean on and grab a drink while we wait.

After half a beer for Mike and half a Riesling for me, Mike pulls me closer. I think he's just going to nuzzle my hair but instead he whispers in my ear. "How'd the waxing appointment go?" Then he leans back with a grin and a twinkle in his eye.

I feel my face heat up as I smile and duck my head away from his gaze. "It went well, thank you," I say. Then I laugh at my stupid formal response. When I glance back up he's smiling too.

It turns out Everly was right. It does feel different

being bare down there. I'm sure I'll get used to the sensation, but I've been slightly turned on since I had it done two days ago. I'm so aware of the weight of my denim jeans over the slip of lace underwear I'm wearing, making me feel a little bold, a little risqué.

Mike tips my chin up with one hand and places a soft kiss on my lips. The other hand is on my hip and his thumb has slipped under my sweater and is resting directly on my heated skin. I'm almost ready to tell him we should ditch the dinner plans and head back to his dorm room when they call us with an available table.

Mike holds my hand and leads me back towards the hostess, then follows me into the restaurant. The hostess seats us at our table, dropping two menus down before departing.

"Thank you." I smile as Mike hands one of the menus to me. Mike flips his menu open and I'm about to do the same when my eyes move to a table slightly behind Mike, to the right.

Luke.

Ten

He's staring directly at me. Our eyes lock as my mind races. My good mood vanishes as I contemplate an entire meal with my gynecologist as chaperone.

"Hi, I'm Brandee." The waitress has arrived. "Can I get you drinks while you look at the menus?"

Mike orders a Coke and I order a second glass of wine. I cross my legs under the table and glance back at Luke. He's still staring at me. He's not smiled in greeting once. Maybe I should smile? I try that. Luke's jaw ticks in response and his lips don't move.

"What are you getting?" Mike asks, redirecting my attention back to him.

I haven't even looked at the menu. I glance down, pretending I've been reviewing it. "Pad Thai." I give Mike a huge smile and close the menu, setting it down on the table. I shift in my seat so I can glance back to Luke's table. Luke's lips are moving now and I notice for the first time he's not alone. There's a beautiful red-haired woman sitting across from him. He's on a date.

She's in a cream sweater dress and tall brown fuck-me boots. I can see them from my vantage point. She looks very elegant though, classy. I'd guess her to be much closer to his age than I am. I'd also guess she doesn't own a single pair of socks that say classy bitch across the bottoms.

"Are you ready to order?" Brandee is back, placing our drinks on the table and pulling out a pen and pad. She smiles and looks between Mike and I. We glance at each other and nod. Brandee jots our order down and stuffs the pad into her apron pocket, promising to be back soon with an appetizer I didn't even catch Mike ordering. I'm a bad date.

I focus on Mike and get him talking. He's majoring in business, and he has a definite plan after graduation. He wants to open a deluxe car wash on the empty lot next to his dad's Chevy dealership and once that's up and running open a custom auto paint shop. He has a business plan ready, something he put together last year for a class, but he's really passionate about it. It might sound silly, but he has a vision for his success. Eventually he'll learn his dad's business and take it over when he retires.

Brandee places an order of chicken satay on our table with a warm smile. "Are you two students at Penn?"

"We are." Mike beams at her. "Are you an alumna?"

"Yes, I am." Brandee nods. "Met my husband there." She smiles at the two of us, like we remind her of her and her spouse. "We'd love for our daughter to attend Penn after high school, but she's determined to attend Penn State. Three hours away!" She shrugs and sighs, like she can't bear the thought of her baby flying so far away from the coop.

"Which building did you live in?" Mike asks her, popping a piece of chicken into his mouth.

"I lived in Frider Hall." She starts to laugh. "We had

this security guard there named Mr Holguin, but he insisted we call him Fireball."

"Fireball!" Mike exclaims. "That guy is still there!"

I sneak another look over to Luke's table while Mike is laughing over the antics of the oldest, most beloved school employee on campus. Their food has arrived. Luke's date is mid-sip on a glass of wine and Luke is placing a forkful of noodles into his mouth. The fingers of his left hand are resting on the wooden table top, inches from a cell phone. His index finger is tapping the wood in a slow steady rhythm.

I look up to his face and find his eyes on mine once again. My heart slows then speeds up. Why does he keep staring at me? I steal a look at Mike—he's still distracted with the waitress. I'm surprised Luke's date hasn't noticed his lack of eye contact, since his eyes seem to be primarily on me.

No sooner do I have that thought than the redhead is half turning in her seat to look me over. She gives me the universal female once-over, as much as she can from her seat. She looks more curious than hostile as she takes me in.

She's stunning. Her makeup is flawless, pale skin, green eyes radiating intelligence and knowledge. Carnal knowledge. These two know each other on a bodily fluids level. I'd love to fool myself into thinking she's Luke's sister, but this woman is definitely not related to Luke. Not siblings. Not half-siblings. Not even step-siblings.

The woman turns back to Luke and says something. He looks at me a moment longer before replying to whatever she said.

"I'll have your entrees out in a few minutes," Brandee

says and moves on to her next table. I grin at Mike and move a chicken satay to the plate in front of me.

"I can't believe old man Fireball has been pulling the same pranks for twenty years," Mike says.

"Twenty? I think he's been at Penn for at least sixty years." I take a bite.

"Yeah," Mike laughs. "I'd like to think he graduated in 1960 and just never left."

I laugh. "I hope that's true. Though you'd think the residents of Frider would warn the new kids each fall."

"Nah," Mike scoffs. "It's like a rite of passage. Besides, the old guy loves to mess with the new kids. He's earned the privilege." Mike grins as my cell phone beeps.

"Oh," I say. "I should check that in case it's my grandparents." I slide the phone from my purse. "The ladder accident this week freaked me out. Seeing my grandfather in a hospital bed was awful. I hate knowing they're getting older." I give Mike a little smile. "You're lucky your parents are a long way off from old age."

"Yeah, I am," he agrees.

I unlock my phone and freeze.

"Grandparents okay?" Mike asks, concerned.

"Yeah," I reply. "Fine." Which is not technically a lie. I assume they're fine because the text is not from them. It's from Luke.

Eleven

Are you going home with him?

I'm so floored, I'm not even sure how to respond.

> Maybe I went home with him last night.
> Maybe we're just refueling in the midst of
> a twenty-four-hour fuck fest, Dr. Miller.

Be careful, Miss Tisdale.

For crying out loud! Why is he texting me? He's on a date! I'm on a date! We are not on the same date! I hit the lock button on my phone and place it face down on the table.

At the next table, Luke's phone rings. He rises from the table and I hear him tell the caller, "This is Dr. Miller," as he walks toward the front of the restaurant. The redhead doesn't seem fazed in the least.

"I'm going to run to the bathroom before the food gets here, babe." Mike walks back towards the hostess stand and disappears from view a moment before

Brandee is back with a fresh glass of wine and our meals.

"Oh, thank you," I frown at the wine. "I didn't order another glass though."

"Your boyfriend did." Brandee smiles warmly at me. She's obviously smitten with Mike, but then, most women are.

I look at the wine and shrug. Oh, well, what the hell. I take a gulp and stare at my food. It would be rude to start without him.

I use the time to check out the redhead again. Their table has been cleared and she's patiently scrolling through her phone waiting for Luke to return.

I take another sip. Mike switched to soda when we sat down. He's so considerate, knowing he's driving and stopping at one drink. He comes across like a bit of a player on campus, but he's a good guy.

Luke's back. He doesn't sit down, just stops at the table, leaning down to say something to his date before straightening and pulling cash from his wallet to toss on the table.

He pulls her chair back and places a hand on her back, guiding her to the front, not even glancing at me as they walk out. What the ever-loving fuck?

He stares at me all night, texts me while on a date with another woman, then walks out of here without a backward glance? *Sophie, get a grip. You're about to walk out of here with Mike, who cares what Dr. Miller does or doesn't do?* What is his deal though? I don't know what to make of him, other than he's a hot doctor who sends a lot of mixed messages.

I take another gulp of wine and tuck my hair behind my ear. I cross and uncross my legs. I'm so aware of my bare pussy. I feel as though half the blood in my body is pulsing right there. I'm achy. I clench, testing the muscles. My whole body feels warm and relaxed. *Let's get this show on the road, Mike.* I shift in my seat again, enjoying the pressure between my thighs as I tighten my crossed legs.

I feel someone move into my personal space and I turn my head, expecting to see Mike leaning in to sneak a kiss. The smile falls off my face as I take in Luke leaning over me.

"Your date had to leave. Get up. I'm driving you home."

My heart starts to pound and my mind races. What is happening? Where did Mike go? Why is Luke involved? Is Mike okay? Did I just get stood up in the middle of a date?

I blink at Luke. I turn back to the table set before me. Our untouched meals sit, no longer steaming, still waiting to be eaten. My eyes rest on my half-finished wine glass. No use wasting that, at least. I pick up the glass and knock it back in one long swallow. Keeping it classy in front of Luke has become my specialty.

He pulls out his wallet and leaves a stack of bills on the table before pulling my chair back. I look up and catch a surprised look on the waitress' face. My cheeks redden in embarrassment. I walked in with one man and I'm walking out with another, who just paid the bill for a meal I never even got to eat. I can't comprehend what's happening right now but I'm more than happy to get out of here and figure it out without an audience.

I slide my phone off the table as I stand, sneaking a glance around. The waitress has busied herself with a table. No one is looking at me, actually. Except a chubby blonde baby in the corner. She's definitely staring at me. Nosy baby.

Luke already has my jacket in his hands. I slide my purse over a shoulder and start walking towards the front. My cell is still clutched in my hand. I flick it alive as I walk and glance at the screen. Maybe Mike tried to reach me with some kind of explanation, but the screen is blank. No new alerts. Do I have a signal? Yes. I open the last text conversation between Mike and I. Maybe there's a text I missed? No. *I'm in the lobby*, was the last message he sent me, ninety minutes ago.

I weave my way through the restaurant to the door, knowing Luke is right behind me. There's a mass of people standing around the front waiting on tables. I glance around, still expecting to see Mike, asking me why I'm leaving.

Maybe he's outside smoking. He doesn't smoke. But it would still make more sense than him just disappearing. I'm racking my brain trying to make sense of this. We were having a good time. The evening was going well. I was a sure thing, dammit! He knew I was going home with him.

I know he didn't chicken out. He didn't turn gay and run out of here. It's not like that could possibly happen to me twice.

We arrive at the restaurant door and Luke reaches around me to open it. His shirt sleeves are pushed up to the elbow and I notice the muscles in his forearm as he pulls the door back, ushering me through. My mind flashes to an hour ago when Mike held the same door open for me. When did this night go so terribly wrong?

The cool air outside awakens me from my shocked stupor. The sidewalk is busy. I take a step out of the way, stopping in front of the window display of the closed shop next door. I shiver and start to wrap my arms around myself to ward off the evening chill. Luke stops directly in front of me and holds up the right sleeve of my jacket, silently instructing me to push my arm through before repeating the gesture with my left.

He pulls the jacket over my shoulders and tugs it closed. The action makes me feel small, like a child. He is standing so close I can make out the tiny fibers of his gray sweater and the scent of his aftershave. He cups my jaw and tilts my head back to meet his gaze.

"You are never seeing that asshole again. Do you understand me, Sophie?"

Twelve

My rage is instantaneous. I place both hands on Luke's chest and shove, only succeeding in dislodging his hand from my face. He doesn't move an inch.

"You're the reason my date disappeared?" I seethe. "What gives you the right?" My heart is beating so fast, my shock and anger an adrenaline rush. Luke is silent, staring at me like I'm a toddler having a tantrum over a denied toy.

Oh, God. I cringe. "I do not have a daddy fetish, you sick fuck!" I hiss at him.

Luke rubs a hand over his face and mutters, "Jesus," before wrapping his hand around my upper arm and physically hauling me towards the street.

He opens the passenger side door of a sleek black sports car parked on the street and has me seated inside before I can object. The door slams shut with barely a sound and I'm surrounded in luxury leather and trim.

Luke slides in next to me, starting the engine and fastening his seatbelt in one smooth movement before glancing at me. "I'll assume since you no longer need a booster seat you can fasten yourself." His eyes flick to my unfastened seatbelt.

Asshole. I yank the seatbelt with more vigor than

necessary and jam it into the buckle. Luke merges the car onto Chestnut heading east. We drive in silence before taking a right onto 38th Street.

"You live on campus, correct?" he asks, breaking the silence.

He really is taking me home. This isn't some alpha-male power play that ends up with me in his bed.

"I was going to sleep with him," I say quietly, not answering his question. "I have your stupid condoms in my purse." I glance at him. Luke's silent, his eyes on the road. I turn my head away and watch the landscape slide past. "It's my choice who I sleep with, Dr. Miller. I'm not sure why you even gave me a bagful of condoms if you're just going to cockblock me from using them."

"Don't call me Dr. Miller."

That's his response? I turn back to look at him. "What did you say to my date, *Luke?*"

Luke glances at me before refocusing on the road. "I told him I'd drive you home."

"Why?" I'm confused. "I don't understand."

Luke glances at me briefly. "It's not important. He's an asshole, Sophie. You deserve better."

"Why?" I demand.

We're nearing campus now and the speed limit drops. The interior of the car is quiet, the ride smooth.

"He was outside on the phone telling his buddy that if he couldn't talk you into making a sex tape tonight he had another girl lined up for later."

"Oh." I need to process that.

"Are you okay?" We're at a stoplight. He's looking at me. The tiny lines around his eyes are creased in concern. I stare back for a second before I erupt, louder than necessary in the silent car.

"I can't believe I waxed for that jerk!"

Luke looks taken aback as the car behind us honks. The light is green.

"I didn't even do it myself! Because apparently waxing yourself is just not done. Did you know that, Luke? I paid someone to give me a Brazilian wax. Do you know how embarrassing that is? To be spread naked on a table in front of a complete stranger? Do you? Wait." I throw my hands up in surrender. "Of course you do. You're a gynecologist. You see naked women in embarrassing positions all day long."

I slump in the passenger seat, placing my elbow on the window sill and resting my head on my hand. "Do all women get turned on when you examine them, Luke?" I don't wait for a reply. "Probably not. Even though you're crazy hot and have no right being a gyno, I bet normal women don't get wet when you walk into the room. I bet they don't go home and get themselves off imagining it's your hand instead of their own." He clears his throat, but I'm on a roll. "There's something wrong with me, Luke. I dated a gay guy for two years and now I have a gynecologist fetish." I give up propping my head up and just lean against the window.

"And I'm a shitty judge of character. I almost gave my virginity to an asshole who was going to record it." I shudder. "Eww." I sit up and twist in my seat towards him. "Do you want it, Luke? Because you can have it." I slide a hand up his thigh until I hit a very noticeable bulge. Hmm, I think someone does want me.

My hand is promptly removed and set back in my lap. Or not.

"Exactly how much have you had to drink tonight, Sophie?"

I cross my arms across my chest, rejected. It's not that far from the restaurants on Chestnut to campus. Luke's been circling the same block while I babbled. "I had a few glasses of wine, but I haven't eaten," I respond defensively. "Someone broke up my date before I had the chance."

"Which building do you live in?" Luke asks, turning right on Sansom Street as he loops the block again.

"I live in Jacobsen. Get back to 38th and then take a left on Spruce Street." I sigh, defeated. "Wait! I can't go back to my room! I told my roommate I wasn't coming back tonight. And Everly's in New York." I start to cry and I feel even more stupid than I did before. Tonight has been a storm of expectations, adrenaline and disappointment. I'm overwhelmed. *It's fine,* I tell myself. *Everything will be fine.* I can have Luke drop me off at the library. I'll find something to read until closing and then text Jeannie. I can sleep in the dorm lobby if I need to.

I'm wiping the tears off my face when I realize we've passed Jacobsen and are heading toward the river, away from campus. "Where are we going?" I ask.

"Home."

Home? His home? I glance at him, confused.

"I'll take you to my place until you can reach your roommate." He glances over at me. "Okay?"

"Yeah. That's fine." I'm silent for a minute. "Thank you." I relax into the seat. The digital clock on the dashboard reads 7:32 pm. I'm tired. A lot has happened in the last two hours. I'm a little buzzed from the wine too, if I'm being honest.

I have no idea where Luke lives, but we've crossed the river and now we're on 18th Street headed towards Rittenhouse Square. I want to ask, but I don't want to say anything to make him second-guess his decision.

"The redhead won't be mad?" Oops. *Real smooth, Sophie.* I chance a quick glance at him and see him smirk.

"No. She won't mind."

"She's not your girlfriend then?" *Shut up, Sophie! Shut up, shut up, shut up!*

"No, Sophie, she's not."

"Oh." I really do shut up then. So she's not his girlfriend, but he still rejected me.

We pass Rittenhouse Square Park on our left and then immediately turn into the parking garage of a high-rise. Luke pulls the car into a numbered space and I hop out as soon as the car is in park. I follow him into an elevator and watch him push the top button for the penthouse. He ignores me, pulling a phone from his pocket and flicking the screen with his thumb. I use the time to observe him. He's wearing gray slacks with a gray sweater. The sweater sleeves are still pushed up to his elbows. Polished black shoes and a chunky watch on his left wrist complete the ensemble.

He glances up and notices me eyeing him. I look away, embarrassed at being so obvious. Thirty-three floors in this building. The doors open onto a marble landing. I'm silent as Luke unlocks the door and ushers me inside. I follow him down a hallway covered in wide-plank dark hardwood. There's a large round entryway that appears to be the center of the condo. The space has one of those round tables in the middle complete with a vase of fresh flowers in the center. I can see a dining table straight ahead and hallways off the circular space to the left and right. Luke turns left and then right into the kitchen.

"Sit."

He doesn't indicate where, so I choose a seat at the island versus the table in front of the windows on the far side of the room. I glance around as he opens and closes cabinet doors. High-end stainless-steel appliances, professionally distressed white cabinets and Carrara marble countertops. It's a gorgeous kitchen. He can't possibly use it. A fact he confirms when he turns to me and asks if I want a peanut butter and jelly sandwich or Italian takeout from the place downstairs.

"Do you have milk?" I ask.

He does that little smirk-smile of his and nods. "I do."

"Peanut butter and jelly then," I say, getting up from my seat.

"Stay." He nods to my seat. "I've got it." He sets a tall glass of cold milk in front of me and slaps two slices of bread on the counter before slathering one side with peanut butter and the other with jelly. I watch him work, intrigued. From the little I've seen of this place, it's enormous. Does he live here alone? Do doctors make this kind of money? I don't think so.

"Do you own this place?"

"I do." He lifts an eyebrow.

"It seems really large for just you." I glance around. "And expensive."

He shrugs. "The top floor came with this much space. And I like to be on top"—he places my sandwich on a plate and slides it over to me—"Sophie."

Okay. That was a definite sexual innuendo. This guy is

all over the place, or a tease.

His phone rings and he glances at it before answering with a terse, "Dr. Miller."

I take a bite and listen to his end of the conversation.

"I'll be there in twenty minutes." He finishes the call and places the cell back in his pocket. "I have to run to the hospital and check on a patient. Make yourself at home. There's a television in the family room." He points to a door on the left. "I should be back in a couple of hours."

"A couple of hours?" I ask, surprised. "Don't babies take longer than that?"

"I don't normally deliver the babies, Sophie." He walks around the granite island and pauses in front of me. "I hate to burst your gynecologist fetish bubble, but I'm a reproductive endocrinologist." He tucks a strand of hair behind my ear and his fingers caress the edge.

I try not to react. Because I want to. I want to lean in and kiss his palm. I want to beg him to do so much more.

"My job is to get the patient pregnant, then I hand them off to an obstetrician."

"So you specialize in knocking women up?"

"Yeah. Rich women or women with great health insurance." He taps the tip of my nose. "Not college students."

"I'm not looking to get knocked up."

"Good. Now finish your sandwich and sober up so I can take you home."

His footsteps fade and the front door clicks shut.

I place my empty plate and glass in the dishwasher before walking into the adjoining family room with the television Luke mentioned. I look around. This place is decorated like an expensive model home. I don't see any indication that anyone really lives here. No magazines or stray mugs on the end tables. I'm not really interested in watching TV, I'm interested in a house tour.

Exiting the family room through a door that connects back to the hallway, I find a study. This room looks lived in. He spends time in here—I can smell his cologne lingering in the air. The walls are lined in books. Mainly medical, but there's a few crime mysteries too. Not a copy of *Fifty Shades of Grey* anywhere, sadly. There's a Mac set up on the desk and some stray pens and paperwork scattered across it.

I leave the study and cross the circular center point of the condo. Skipping a massive formal living and dining room, I follow the dark hardwood floor back towards the front door. There's a hallway to the left and right of the front door. I investigate the space to the left first. Three virtually identical bedrooms with their own adjoining baths. They're all empty. As in, completely empty. The same hardwood floor runs wall to wall in each. Not a bed, dresser or hanger in the closets.

The hallway to the right of the door leads me to a massive coat closet and laundry room. I pass both in favor of the door at the end, the master bedroom. There's a walk-in closet the size of my dorm room on my left. It's empty. This is starting to get a little creepy. He does live here, right? He didn't just abandon me in a vacant condo. No, his office looked lived in. I continue and find an even larger walk-in closet across from the master bath. This closet is filled. Rows of neatly organized suits and shirts. Shelves of sweaters and racks of polished shoes.

The bathroom could accommodate a dozen college students, but there's only a vanity for two, an enormous oval tub and a walk-in shower. The entire room is spotless, save for a can of shave cream and a razor on the vanity.

Back in the bedroom there's an area rug covering the hardwood, centering the room and surrounding the massive king-sized bed. I walk back to the bed and open the nightstand drawer. Empty. I cross to the other side, closest to the bathroom, and open that one. Condoms. I sit on the edge of the bed. So he lives in this massive space and uses two rooms of it. A place a doctor could not afford, department head at the hospital or not.

I liked Luke better when he was less confusing, when he was just Luke who flirted subtly with me while buying coffee. That's not true—I like this Luke too. The one who watches out for me and rescues me from a disastrous ending to my date and makes me a sandwich. I like him. I don't like the mixed signals he sends, but I like him.

This bed is really comfortable and I want nothing more than to lie down and close my eyes, so after removing my boots, I do. I can't get comfortable though, so I stand up and strip off my jeans and sweater and climb under the sheets. This bed is heavenly. I hit the light and snuggle into the pillow that smells of Luke. I don't care if he finds me here in my underwear, asleep. I'm tired of his confusing behavior and besides, he's already seen me in less.

Thirteen

I awaken and look at the bedside clock. It's just past eleven. The house is dark and I need to use the bathroom. The air is chilly when I slip out from under the covers, so I wrap a throw from the bed around me as I walk. I make use of the facilities and then wipe off the mascara that's flaked off during my nap and, finding some mouthwash, rinse my mouth before walking back to the bed.

I thought he'd be back by now. I consider lying down again, but I'm wide awake. Maybe I'll watch TV, or find a book in the study. I turn and jump a foot. "Jesus, Luke!"

He's sitting in an armchair in the corner of the room, wide awake, just watching me.

"I was watching you sleep." I love his voice. It's so smooth and deep and embodies control.

"You're a little creepy, you know that?" I ask.

He shrugs. "I come home to find your clothes in a pile on the floor and you asleep in my bed. What should I have done, Sophie?"

I walk towards him. "Joined me?" I suggest.

He smiles at that. "You're twenty-one."

"Yeah." I stop in front of him. "Three years past legal."

"You're a virgin."

"Yeah." That stings. Am I not experienced enough for him? "You want me to come back when I know what I'm doing?" Tears prick at my eyes. I am so sick of the rejection. I toss the throw at him and walk back to my clothes. "Take me home, Luke. I'm sure I can find someone on campus to spend the night with," I say, picking my sweater off the floor. "Believe it or not, plenty of guys on campus would be happy to fuck me without so much conversation about it."

When I stand up he's behind me, his hands on my shoulders. He slides my bra straps over my shoulders before unsnapping it.

"Shut up, Sophie. I don't want to hear another word out of your flippant mouth about you sleeping with some idiot boy on campus. You want me to fuck you, sweetheart? Is that what you want?"

"Yeah." I tilt my head back onto his shoulder. "It is."

"I'm not going to call you in the morning." He's sliding my panties down my legs. "I'm not that guy."

"Okay," I agree.

Holy shit. This is happening. I am finally going to have sex. Luke is not rejecting me again. He's not my gay boyfriend. He's not my jerk boyfriend. He's real and this is happening, right now.

He's bent behind me, pulling the panties free from my ankles before placing his hands on my hips and kissing the curve of my back where it meets my behind. His hands slide lower to cup my ass and his thumbs spread out, caressing me. "Perfect little ass." He's raining kisses over my behind as he speaks. "Do you have any idea how much I've enjoyed eyeing this ass when you turn around to fill my coffee every week?"

I assume his question is rhetorical and remain quiet until he smacks my behind hard with his open palm. "Answer me."

I feel a rush of wetness in my pussy from the slap. What the hell? Why does that make me wet? My ass is still stinging where he smacked me. "No, I didn't know you were thinking about my ass." It's a little hard getting the words out, I'm so distracted by everything. His mouth, his hands, the pressure building between my legs. "I didn't think you even remembered my name week to week. I assumed you were just reading my name tag."

His thumbs pinch into my butt cheeks and spread them as he licks up the crease of my ass. Oh my God.

He turns me so I'm facing him. "Sit." He's pressing on the top of my thighs till my butt hits the edge of the bed. "Cup your tits, Sophie." I do, immediately. They're warm in my own hands, full, my nipples hard. Luke spreads my thighs and moves between them. "Pinch your nipples, play with them." Our eyes lock as I obey.

"I seem to recall you mentioning a fascination with my fingers earlier," he says as he runs his index finger down my crease.

"Oh, God." I flop back onto the bed, mortified that he's bringing that up, and focus my eyes on the ceiling. But I don't let go of my breasts, continuing to caress them as he talks.

"Is it a fascination with my hands as a whole?" He slides both palms under my thighs and caresses them up and down before lifting my legs until my knees are bent and my feet are on the edge of the bed, parallel to my bottom, then he pushes outward so I'm splayed open in front of him. "Or is it a fascination with a specific finger?" He places the tip of a finger inside my entrance and rims the opening. "Or is it my thumb, Sophie?" His breath is hot against my skin as he speaks. "Do you imagine my thumb in your ass as I fuck you from behind?" His thumb is moving across my tightened bud. "Which is it, Sophie? Which of those things did you fantasize about?"

He slaps my pussy, splayed open in front of him, hard. I moan as I feel my own wetness leak out of me. "What did I tell you about answering me?" he demands. "What did you think about when you got yourself off?"

"I thought about all of it," I admit. "Except the thumb thing, that never occurred to me. But I'm open to it," I add.

"You filthy girl," he murmurs, before I feel his hands under my thighs again, holding me open as his tongue makes a long wet swipe over my pussy. My thighs tighten reflexively but he's got me pinned open and rims my asshole with his tongue too.

"Luke!"

He laughs and circles my clit with the tip of his finger, around and around. I can feel more wetness pooling as he moves the tip of his finger inside of me and repeats the rimming motion, stretching me with his fingertip. His tongue travels back to my clit and he circles around the bundle of nerves until I think I will go insane. "I like this pussy bare, Sophie," he says between circles. I'm whimpering and making all sorts of crazy sounds that would mortify me if I had any control right now. "So naughty." His mouth covers my entire mound and I about lose my mind. "If I was keeping you I'd keep this pussy naked and filled with my dick every day. Did you wonder if I could get you off using just my finger?" He's pinching my clit between his finger and thumb as he talks.

"I didn't wonder about that, I was really confident you could," I manage to respond, but I sound like I just sprinted up a flight of stairs.

He slides his finger inside of me and then out, sliding two back in. "Fuck." He sounds gruff. "You feel so good." He slides his fingers out, then in, then widens them, stretching me. "You're so fucking tight, I can't wait to slide my cock inside of you." He slides his fingers in again, then back out, this time adding his thumb to my clit. "So wet. I wanted to finger the fuck out of you on my exam table. Is that what you want to hear? That I was as affected as you were?"

"Yes."

"I had to fight an erection when you came on my finger during the exam. That was a definite first for me Sophie."

"Sorry about that," I manage to gasp out, my back arching on the bed.

"I'm going to fuck you hard, Sophie." He's stroking his fingers in and out. A second later he slams the two fingers back in and curves them as his thumb rubs my clit and I explode. Holy fuck. His fingers continue their magic through my orgasm as he kisses the inside of my thighs.

That was the most intense orgasm of my life. I thought I had orgasms before, when I got myself off, but those were a joke in comparison to what Luke just did to me. I'm still feeling aftershocks rippling through me in waves.

He stands, leaning over me and resting his weight on his hands on either side of me as his mouth fastens around a nipple. I arch my back off the bed. These sensations are too much. I want to push him away and grasp him closer all at the same time.

My heart starts to race with nerves before he slides a hand behind my neck and kisses me. This man can kiss. None of the timid half-assed kisses or frantic kisses I'm used to from college boys. He knows what he's doing and his confidence is addicting, reassuring. I wrap my arms around his neck and run my hands into his hair and I'm afraid I might melt, he feels so good.

He scoots me back all the way onto the bed before standing and pulling his sweater off over his head. My eyes move over his chest as he unzips his pants and they drop to the floor. He's wearing dark briefs and his erection springs free as he drops them. He grabs himself, running his hand up and down the length of him. I squirm a little. He's big. Bigger than Scott and I only had him in my mouth.

Luke looks at me and laughs. I've crossed my legs while I watched him touch himself. He kneels on the bed, separating my legs and lying between them.

He pulls my hand to him and wraps it around his cock, stroking our joined hands up and down, indicating what he wants before he moves his hand to my breast, rolling a nipple between his fingers.

We go back to kissing and I rub my thumb over the tip of him. He's rock hard. My thumb runs across his pre-ejaculate and I rub it in circles with the pad of my thumb across the head. "Sophie," he's chanting between kisses.

He palms both sides of my face and kisses me until I'm breathless before moving one hand to my clit and using the perfect amount of friction until I'm so wet and wanting I'm ready to beg him for more, but I don't need to because he's reaching over me into the nightstand for a condom. The package is opened and the condom rolled on with a practiced ease I don't want to consider.

My heart is racing so fast I'm sure he can hear it. This is what I want. This is what I fantasized about. But I'm slightly terrified all the same.

I tense as he lines himself between my legs and force myself to relax as the head of him nudges inside. I blow out the air I've been holding as he inches slightly inside of my body.

"Look at me." I realize I've had my eyes squeezed shut, which is silly. I'm having sex! Finally! I need to take in every moment of this so I can replay it in my mind forever. "Wrap your arms around my neck." I do and he nudges forward more. Fuck. It burns so bad. He's too big.

"You're too big."

He smirks at that. "I'd say that you're too tight, but there's no such thing to a man." He slides back and forth just inside of me. I know he's nowhere near all the way in. I slide my hands into his hair, feeling the thick strands under my fingers, reveling in being this close to him, able to examine the flecks in his brown eyes from the moonlight lighting the room.

He moves a hand to my clit and rubs it, causing me to relax my muscles, and then thrusts his hips forward all the way.

That feels... horrible, actually. I scrunch my eyes

closed and turn my head away.

"Sophie, Sophie, Sophie." He's kissing my closed eyelids, turning my head back to him. "Open your eyes, doll."

I do, and realize I've got both palms against his chest, trying to physically push him off of me. He kisses me again and I stop pushing and put my arms back around his neck, pulling him closer.

"Your pussy is gripping me so fucking tight."

"It's too tight." I exhale.

"How's this part?" he asks, kissing my neck. "Not quite what you thought?"

"You're just so much bigger than I fantasized."

His chest shakes and his lips move across my jaw. "And you're every man's fantasy with your dirty talk and you're not even trying."

I smile at this and pull his lips to mine and then test moving my hips a little. He follows my lead that I'm ready for more and withdraws before sinking back in. "Hmm, that's good." I sigh.

"You're so fucking sweet." He withdraws and thrusts. "It makes me want to do things to you, Sophie. Filthy things." He twists my nipple as he moves inside of me. "It makes me want to shove my cock down your throat"—he kisses me there—"until you gag on me."

I grab his jaw and kiss him, our tongues wrangling and thrusting in rhythm to his cock thrusting between my thighs. He's so deep his balls slap against my ass as he bangs into me.

"I want to come all over your tits"—he slaps one—"and then smear it all over your chest until it dries." He pulls my left leg up, hanging it over his elbow, changing the penetration. I gasp as he thrusts. It feels different this way. "I want to shove things in your ass." He groans and licks a line of sweat trickling between my breasts and I arch my back, allowing him better access. "I'd start with my thumb, Sophie." He withdraws and slams back in. It's so tight, the friction is making me insane. "But I wouldn't be satisfied until you were bent over and my dick was in your ass."

I come undone then. And this, the feeling of coming stretched around his cock, is like nothing I could have imagined.

I'm so tight after coming, it's a fine line between enjoyment and pain as Luke thrusts again. He exhales above me, his breath ragged with exertion as he comes himself. And *that*, hearing him come while inside of me, feeling his breath against the side of my face on each exhale, that is something I will never forget.

Fourteen

"That guy keeps staring at you," Everly murmurs to me as she wipes down the counter at Grind Me.

"Does he?" I respond, not interested. Random guys hanging out in coffee shops do not concern me.

"He's probably a security detail hired by Dr. Miller to ensure your safety." Everly eyes him from behind the bakery case.

I pause and look at her. "You just said so many ridiculous things I'm not sure where to begin responding."

"Oh, take your time." Everly hops onto the back counter.

I laugh. "Okay, one, that man out there is not anyone's security detail." Everly shrugs so I continue. "Two, I'm not in any danger. And three, Luke isn't doing anything for me. We didn't leave things like that."

Everly examines the French manicure left over from her brother's wedding last weekend as she responds. "One"—she eyes the kid sitting alone by the window—"truth. Two, in romance novels the heroine is always in danger. Three, there's no way Luke is done with you."

"You do realize we are not in a romance novel, right? Besides which, when did you become a romantic?" I raise a skeptical eyebrow at Everly. "Did you catch a bouquet of unicorns at the wedding?"

Everly sighs and crosses her arms across her chest. "No, I didn't catch anything at the wedding except Finn's house key."

"Professor Camden gave you his house key? I though you said he was going to require additional convincing before, and I quote, he accepted what was best for him?"

She waves a dismissive hand. "No, I made myself a copy."

"Everly, no." I am shaking my head at her in disbelief. "No, you did not. How? Does he know?"

"Sophie, it's like you don't even know me. I borrowed his car." She stops at the look on my face. "Fine, I stole his car and ran over to Home Depot and made copies while he was busy with his best man duties."

"No," I'm still shaking my head.

"Yes." She's nodding hers.

"Excuse me?" We both turn to see the guy Everly envisioned as my security detail at the counter. "Can I get a refill?" He holds up his empty mug. At Grind Me we offer free refills on coffee during the same visit.

"Sure." I refill the mug and hand it back. He stares at me for a second longer than I'm comfortable with, but it happens so fast I wonder if I imagined it.

"Back to Luke," Everly states when the guy turns away with his freshly filled mug. I look at her and shrug.

"He said he wouldn't call and I said okay."

"Then he fucked you silly."

"Then he fucked me silly," I agree. And I can't stop the smile that spreads across my face.

"You lucky bitch."

I try to hide another grin, but she's right. It was pretty incredible and far exceeded any expectations I had for my first time. I feel myself blush remembering the feel of him under my fingertips, the way his chest had felt under my head when I'd collapsed on him after and lain there listening to his heartbeat while he'd wound his fingers in my hair.

I like him. I've liked him for weeks, but he didn't promise me anything. I want more, obviously, but life has taught me to be cautious with my expectations. I'm not aggressive like Everly. That girl is a force of nature. I'd feel bad for Professor Camden if I didn't love Everly so much because the girl is a ruthless ninja hidden in a teeny-tiny five-four Playboy Bunny-worthy frame. Her shiny black hair is swinging in a pony tail halfway down her back. Her huge green eyes are always ablaze with a mixture of sincerity and mischief. Professor Camden doesn't stand a chance.

"Sophie, he's going to be back for more. Trust me."

I load a tray of cupcakes and slide them into the bakery case. "I don't know, Everly. He's really sophisticated and clearly lives a lifestyle a long ways from Cowbell Lane," I say, referencing my grandparents' home in Willow Grove.

"Bitch, please. The guy is pushing forty and you're a hot co-ed with a brand-new tight, shiny pussy. He'll be back."

My eyes widen. "Everly, Jesus!"

"Just saying." She holds her hands up in mock defense before breaking into a huge grin.

"You don't really think he's forty, do you?"

"He just turned thirty-six in August."

"How do you know that?"

"Google."

"You Googled him?"

"You didn't?" Everly looks aghast.

"Uh, no." Truthfully I thought about it, but I didn't want to get any more invested in him than I already am.

"Well, look what the pussy dragged in." Everly is smirking.

"Everly, that's not the saying. It's 'cat.' 'Look what the cat dragged in.'"

"Oh, I think I've got the saying right. He's here."

My stomach explodes in nerves as I glance towards the door. Luke is here. I wondered if he'd stick to his normal Tuesday routine and stop here for coffee. I've figured out this Grind Me location is between his Rittenhouse Square condo and the student clinic, but it's hardly the only route he could take or stop he could make.

My heart is beating so fast as I take him in. Is he going to speak to me or go back to just ordering coffee and leaving like he has the last several weeks?

He's in a navy suit today, crisp white shirt and a silvery blue tie. And then my heart stops beating so fast. There's a hand on his arm. I follow that hand to the redhead from Saturday night.

Fifteen

I manage to make it through the rest of my shift while Everly shoots me worried glances.

"Is that the same redhead?" she whispered to me when they walked in, once she realized Luke wasn't alone.

Everly insists it didn't mean anything, that he was eyeing me the entire time while I rang them up and avoided looking at him. But Everly missed the redhead's comment when she turned to fill two large cups of dark roast, room for cream on one.

"She's a barista, Lucas? How darling."

I was still reeling from Luke ordering for her, knowing what she wanted without having to ask her. Her comment was an added slap in the face.

"Gina, stop." That's all he said. I felt his stare on me, but I just dumped his change in the tip jar, not even bothering to ask him if he wanted it, then beamed a huge fake smile to the girl in line behind them and requested her order.

I like Luke. I believed him when he said the redhead wasn't his girlfriend. I believed him when he said he wasn't going to call too. He didn't promise me anything.

But I don't like thinking he's such an ass that he'll walk into Grind Me with the very same woman he was on a date with before he slept with me three nights ago. Not cool. Do I want more time with Luke? Who wouldn't? I don't need a comparison fuck to know that it will be years before I find a lover who will compare to Luke. So sure, I want more of Luke's time, but my expectations are a dinner spent at the same table and a few new sexual positions, not a key to his apartment.

But today's stop at Grind Me with Gina in tow? I never saw that coming. He's arrived alone every Tuesday morning for weeks and today he brings her? Ass.

If he's trying to drive his point home about Saturday being a one-time thing, his message is received loud and clear. But I still can't regret a moment of it.

I skip the campus bus in favor of a very long walk after work. My cheeks are chilled as I make my way down Spruce Street toward Jacobsen Hall. A week ago today was my clinic appointment. For a girl who likes to plan, I sure didn't plan on Luke walking into that exam room or anything that happened after.

My feet crunch over the leaves falling to the sidewalk and I stuff my cold hands into my pockets. Fine, I'm a little pissed. And sad. I'm a practical girl, I wasn't looking for a fairy tale, but I don't feel satisfied by the way this ended with Luke. Sexually, yeah, it was a satisfying experience. Emotionally, it was a little lacking.

Suck it up, Sophie, you got what you wanted.

My phone rings and I slide it out of my pocket and answer as I walk.

"Sophie, honey, it's Gram. I just wanted to let you know that we accepted the offer on the house and our offer on the condo we wanted in Florida was accepted. We're moving!"

I smile. "That's great, Grandma. I'm glad you're finally doing it."

"The buyers want to close on our house here the week before Thanksgiving."

Oh.

"So we've only got four weeks to pack everything up. We're thinking we'll drive down to Florida then, so we don't have to put everything into storage. We can close on the condo in Islamorada the week prior because it's vacant and the owners want to close fast."

I know what she's really asking. She wants to know if I'll be okay without seeing them for Thanksgiving. They've put off retiring for just this reason. They wanted to be nearby for me. "Grandma, it's fine. I can go home with Jeannie or Everly for Thanksgiving."

"Are you sure? We can get you a plane ticket if you want to fly down for the long weekend."

"Yes, I'm sure. It's fine, I'm sure you'll have plenty to do with unpacking and friends to see." They have good friends who retired to the area several years ago.

"We already have invitations from the Mirabellis and the Blackwells to get together as soon as we get to town." Grandma sounds thrilled and I'm happy for her. "You'll come down for Christmas though, right? We'll have a room ready for you."

I agree that Florida for Christmas sounds like a great idea and we say our goodbyes as I reach the front door of Jacobsen.

There's a black Mercedes S63 parked illegally in the loading zone. And leaning against it, watching me, is Luke.

"You're here for me?" I gesture to myself with the

hand still holding the phone.

"Yeah, you." He rubs his bottom lip with his thumb, a movement so simple yet so erotic, before placing his hands in his pockets.

I don't reply. I'm not sure what I'm supposed to say. We stare at each other in silence. He takes a step towards me and I instinctively take a step back, then rock forward on my toes.

"You said you wouldn't call," I finally say. My voice has a bitchier tone than I intended.

"I didn't call." His voice is unapologetic.

I want to roll my eyes. "No. You brought your date to my workplace instead." The wind whips a piece of hair into my face and it sticks to my lip gloss. I swipe the hair away and move a step to the left, using his body to block the wind. He's so much bigger than me. The thought fills my head with memories of how he felt over me.

"She wasn't supposed to be there." He steps closer again.

"What does that even mean?" I take a step back and bump into his car. We've danced around and switched positions. He pulls his hands from his pockets and places them on the roof of the low-slung car on either side of me, pinning me in place. I have to tilt my head back to look him in the eye.

"I can't stop thinking about you, Sophie." His eyes search my face. "This morning was... wrong. It's all wrong. You're too young for me. You're sweet and unspoiled." He swipes another errant hair off my cheek and tucks the hair behind my ear. "I should leave you the hell alone, let you find someone more suitable, but I feel selfish about you." He places his hand back on the roof and leans in. "What do you want, Sophie?" he breathes into my ear.

I shiver and it's not from the cold. He smells so good and he looks even better. The cars pass us on Spruce Street while I think, the front doors of Jacobsen slamming open and closed.

"Sophie, I'm not talking to myself. I asked you a question and I expect a response. What do you want?"

"You." I look at him, finally. "I want you."

Sixteen

Luke has me in the passenger seat of his car the second I agree I want him, and at his condo about fifteen minutes after that. We don't speak the entire car ride, but I know where we're going and why.

He doesn't touch me in the elevator. It's empty, but he never lays a finger on me. Instead, we talk.

"Are you sore?"

I've been staring politely at my toes, leaning against the opposite elevator wall. I raise my eyes to his. "Um, yes."

"How sore?" He smirks now, running his eyes up and down my body.

I look away. "A little sore." I meet his eyes again. "But much better than the last two days," I say, in case he's thinking we can't have sex right now.

He nods. "Better than the next two days will be as well."

Okay, no worries, then. I smile at him and clear my throat.

"What time is your afternoon class?"

"Two o'clock."

He checks his watch. "I'd like to see your sweet little mouth wrapped around my cock. Should we start with that today?"

"I've sucked cock before, Luke. I'm not *that* innocent." Does he think I know nothing?

He raises an eyebrow at me. "Sophie," he says sharply.

"What?" Now I'm confused.

He crosses the elevator and places his forearm on the wall over my head. He's standing so close that I have to look up at him. I'm cornered but he's still not touching me. "A word to the wise, Miss Tisdale. I have no interest in hearing about any cocks you've sucked prior to mine. It would behoove you to never mention it again."

"Maybe I'm good at it," I suggest, looking him in the eye. "Maybe you'll be happy with my experience?"

He slams his forearm against the elevator wall over my head before stepping back. He glances at the elevator panel and then back to me. "Do you want me to strip those tiny jeans off your body? Bend you over my knee? You want my palm slapping against your ass till it turns bright pink? Until my fingers slip between your thighs to test how wet you are? Is that what you're after?"

"I, uh," I stammer. "I don't know. Maybe?" I'm getting wet hearing him describe it so I'd probably like it.

The elevator doors open on floor thirty-three and Luke stands with his arm on the door waiting for me to exit. I do so and he lands a playful smack on my ass as I pass him.

"Hey!" I object.

He unlocks the door and holds it open for me. I grin and walk backwards into the apartment, protecting my behind.

"Bedroom."

"You're not going to make me a sandwich first this

time?"

"Now." He's loosening his tie and walking towards me.

I walk backwards as I remove my jacket. "Should I hang this up?" I smile and nod towards the front hall closet we're passing. He removes the jacket from my hand and tosses it on the floor.

I bite my lip to keep from laughing before I turn and head for the bedroom, pulling the shirt I wore to work off over my head as I walk. My bra hits the floor as I pass the doorway into the bedroom. My hands reach for the button on my jeans before Luke stops me. He sits on the edge of the bed and beckons me over.

He circles my waist with his hands before pulling a nipple into his mouth. Oh, God, he feels so good. I wrap my hands around his head, running my fingers through his hair, pulling him closer.

"I decided I did want to take these off myself." His fingers move to the button on my jeans. His hands seem enormous working the button free, but he does it with ease before sliding the zipper down. It's hot watching him undress me. He moves his hands to my sides and wiggles the denim over my hips before the jeans drop to the floor.

"Bend over." He pats his knee.

Okay, we're really doing this? I look at his face. He's serious. I bend over his knee, the position perfect for my clit to rub against his leg. This is nice. I grin with my head upside down, my hands resting on the floor.

"These are cute." He's rubbing his hand over my underwear. I'm wearing a pair of plain black cotton panties. "Not as cute as your ass though." He slaps me hard before pulling the panties down to mid-thigh.

Not gonna lie, that felt nice. He smooths his hand over my ass in circular strokes. "Don't antagonize me, Sophie." His hand comes down against my skin in a crack. I jump a little, but I enjoy it.

"Okay," I sigh. "I'll try not to." I grin at him over my shoulder. "But this is kinda nice, so maybe I'll antagonize just a little?"

Luke groans and slaps my behind hard three times. That stings. He goes back to smoothing his palm in circles, taking away the burn.

"You're a little handful, aren't you, Sophie?" he asks as he delivers another smack.

"I'm really not," I disagree. "I'm a very good girl, normally." I shift on his lap, grinding my clit against his thigh.

He spanks me again and again before sliding his fingers into me from behind. "You enjoyed that too much." He's dragging his fingers in and out as he speaks.

"I'm sorry," I apologize, still hanging upside down.

He laughs and smacks my ass again. "Get up."

I stand and finish removing my undies—they've been mid-thigh this entire time. He's watching me and unbuttoning his pants, his meaning clear. His loosened tie still hanging from his neck catches my attention. I reach forward and slip it over his head. "Can I tie you?" I'm really excited about this idea.

He looks at me skeptically as he unbuttons his shirt and shrugs it off. He stands and drops his pants and I swear saliva pools in my mouth looking at him. "Sure." He shrugs. "What'd you have in mind?"

I grin and indicate he should lie on the bed and then

tie his hands to the headboard. "You know," I drawl, "I've never done this before." I bat my eyelashes at him from between his legs. "I think it will help my confidence with you restrained." He laughs, playing along.

I sit back on my heels between his thighs and place a fingertip coyly on my lip. I grasp him with the other hand, sliding my hand up and down the length of him. "You want me to put this in my mouth?" I'm all wide-eyed innocence.

He's propped up on some pillows, his wrists attached to the headboard with his tie. A big grin crosses his face. I like seeing him happy. Most of our encounters have been fraught with tension. This is different, nice.

"I do want that, Sophie." He groans when I add a second hand, cupping his balls gently. "I want that very much." His voice has already grown husky.

I massage his sack with my hand while stroking the length with the other. "I don't know." I bite my lip. "I've never done anything like this before." I twist my wrist as I stroke upwards. "I'm not sure I know what to do."

Luke blows out a breath. "Wrap your impertinent little lips around my cock. I'm pretty sure you can figure out the rest."

"Okay, I'll try." I lean forward, leaving one hand on his cock and resting my weight on the other. I lick the base of his penis before sucking on his balls and rubbing my thumb back and forth on the underside of his cock.

"Jesus, Sophie."

Pre-come oozes from the tip so I slide my hand up and catch it with my thumb, massaging the moisture in circles across his skin. I move my mouth to the base of his cock where my thumb was and repeat stroking the underside with my tongue.

I tighten the grip of my fingers around the head just slightly and continue rubbing my thumb across the tip as I lick up the length of him until I reach my hand.

I look up at Luke. His face is strained, his breathing fast. I make eye contact with him as I drag the hand circling the tip of him down his shaft in a slow, firm stroke. Then finally I take him into my mouth.

"Christ, Sophie." He groans and closes his eyes but immediately opens them again to watch. I love this. I can feel my own wetness leaking, I'm so turned on doing this to him. I bob down the length of him and sneak a hand to my clit, rubbing myself. This is such a power trip. Beside me his legs tense and above me he's giving a running commentary on my filthy little tongue and wicked little fingers.

It feels good to be in charge of him, just momentarily. He's bigger, older and stronger, but right now, I'm in control. It feels empowering.

I slide a finger inside of myself. I think I could get off doing this but I've got something else in mind right now. I rest my weight on my knees so I can use both hands, then increase my efforts stroking his cock below the amount I can take in my mouth.

He's close. I know he's close. Mainly because he says, "Sophie, I'm going to come in your mouth if you don't stop." As if I'd stop.

I've never swallowed before but I want to now. I want him in my mouth when he explodes. I want to swallow down everything he can give me. He's very supportive once he realizes I'm not stopping. "Sophie, you filthy bitch, I'm going to come so hard down your throat."

When I think he can't hold out any longer I take my finger, slick with my own wetness, and slide it into his ass.

He comes.

A lot.

"You hussy, Sophie." He winds his hands in my hair as I swallow and then flips us over so he's on top.

"Hey, I tied you!" I object from under a wall of muscle.

"With a bow tie, Sophie." He holds my face between his hands and kisses me until I'm short on oxygen. "You're so sweet. What the hell am I going to do with you?" He pauses then, searching my eyes like this is an actual question, so I answer.

"Keep me."

He doesn't respond. Instead, reaching for a condom, he flips my legs up so I'm damn near bent in half and slides into me.

I squirm a little. This is still so new to me and he's so damn big. "How are you even ready to go again?" I question.

"My dick is in a permanent state of ready when you're in the room," he responds, while still sliding into me.

"That must have been awkward for you with me spread out on your exam table." I wrap my arms around his neck and kiss whatever skin I can reach.

"You have no idea."

I laugh. "I think I do."

"By the way"—he moves my right leg to his shoulder and sinks back into me—"I can't be your doctor anymore."

"Hmmm, okay." God, he feels so good. How in the hell did I wait this long to have sex? "We can still play doctor though, right? I'm into it."

"Fucking hell, Sophie." He slaps my behind and I come. He slows his thrusts while I recover, thrusting his tongue into my mouth in rhythm with his cock.

When my muscles are done contracting he withdraws, turns me on my side and drops my upper leg over his arm, re-entering me from behind. He slams into me while rubbing my clit. Oh.

"You mean we're not done?" I ask, confused.

He laughs and nips my ear with his teeth. "No."

"But last time you just came when I did." It's getting hard to get my point across with his fingers working me so expertly.

"Last time I went easy on you, beautiful." He kisses my neck.

"But I thought the goal was to finish?"

"That's the goal"—his balls are slapping against my skin as he thrusts—"when you've got kids screaming in the other room." He hikes my thigh a little higher on his arm. "It's not the goal with your new lover."

He shows me then just how good he is at long-term goals.

Seventeen

"This place is dead." Everly yawns.

"It's two days before Thanksgiving. I think a lot of people took the week off work." I take a sip of the chai tea latte I just made myself. We're at work and Everly is right, it's slow.

"Your stalker didn't take the week off." Everly nods to the guy at a table, wearing an earbud and ignoring us.

I ignore her statement. "Why aren't you in Connecticut already? We don't have classes this week."

Everly rolls her eyes. "I'm stuck here until tomorrow because Finn is waiting until the last minute to go home. He thinks if he waits long enough I'll take the train and he won't have to drive me." She shrugs. "Sometimes I'm not sure why I put up with him."

"What exactly are you putting up with? You're the one stalking him."

She sticks a cup under the syrups and pumps out several. Experimenting with drink concoctions is a Everly specialty. They're mostly awful. "It's not stalking when we are meant to be together. I can't help it that I imprinted on him when I was six."

I spit my drink out. "Everly, did you just use a *Twilight* reference to explain your obsession with Professor

Camden?"

"I did." She pauses from her drink-making. "Is that weird?"

"Um, let's see, *Twilight* wasn't written yet when you were six," I start.

Everly scoffs and turns back to the syrups. "That doesn't mean it didn't happen."

"And you're not a werewolf," I add before she can object.

"Whatever."

That's the sum total of her response on the subject. I watch her add steamed milk to her cup. "That reminds me, does Professor Camden know that you copied his house key yet?"

"Yeah, he already took the first copy back," Everly replies and continues making her drink.

I have to set my latte down at that point. I should know better than to have a conversation with Everly while drinking hot liquids. "The first copy, Everly?"

"Yeah. And he didn't even ask me for the second copy." She takes a sip of her drink. "I'm kind of pissed off about it, to be honest. It's like he doesn't even know me, right?"

I nod slowly. "Right."

"Obviously I would make three copies. Anyone should know that."

I lean against the back counter and nod. "Obviously." Honestly, I have no idea how many copies one would make when stealing someone's house key, but it's best to just go along when Everly is on a roll.

"I expect him to change his locks once I use the second key so the third key is likely useless, but he should know me well enough to ask for the second key." She sighs, looking truly despondent.

"Everly, why Professor Camden? Men trip over themselves trying to get to you. Why him?"

"He's the one, Sophie. He just is."

"Why now?" I ask, confused. "I've known you since freshman year and I didn't even know you knew him outside of school until a month ago."

"I had to wait until the time was right. I knew there was no way he was touching me before I was eighteen, just no way." She shakes her head. "I could have gone to college anywhere and focused on bumping into him after I graduated, but I figured if I went to school here I could keep an eye on him. Make sure he didn't fall in love with the wrong girl while I was growing up."

I sigh. "Everly, how were you going to prevent that?" I hold up a hand. "Wait, I don't want to know."

"And then I'd have all senior year to make him realize I was the one for him. That was my plan, you know?" She looks to me for a response.

"That's a plan all right." I have no idea how that is a plan.

"But he's turning out to be a real hard-ass about university policy. I'm not even in any of his classes. Who cares, right?"

"I think the university cares."

"It's not like I'm expecting him to date me openly before June, but there is no reason he can't fuck me before then."

Everly is obviously incredulous at Finn's refusal to fornicate with her. No need to add insult to injury. "Nope, none," I agree.

The front door opens and with it comes a rush of cold air.

"Luke!" I round the counter and stop in front of him. "I didn't think I'd see you here today." I'm grinning, I'm so happy to see him. I should play it cooler, I suppose. I'm still not entirely sure what we are to each other. I got what I wanted—in the last month we've had several meals at the same table and he's taught me several new positions in bed. And in the bathroom. And in the study too. Oh, God, the study. My eyes glaze a little thinking about it.

Luke leans in and kisses me. "What are you thinking about, precious?" he says just loud enough for me to hear.

"Just thinking about your study." I smirk. "It's such a nice room, that's all." He swats my ass and I jump. "You're obsessed with my ass, perv." I slip back behind the counter. "Do you want a coffee? I can wiggle my ass while I pour it."

"Sure."

I fill a large cup with the Grind Me dark roast blend and set it on the counter. "So what are you doing here today? Isn't the student clinic closed all week?"

"I wanted to see you before you left." He smiles at me.

I frown. "Where am I going?" I ask.

Now it's his turn to frown. "I thought you were going to Florida for Thanksgiving weekend?"

"No." I shake my head. "I'm going to Florida next month for Christmas. I'm going home with my roommate Jean for Thanksgiving Day."

"Come home with me."

"Come home with you? Now?"

"No, Thursday. Come to Thanksgiving with me. At my parents'. Unless you'd rather go to Jean's?"

"I'd rather be with you," I answer easily.

Luke leaves after that while Everly mutters, "Shiny new pussy," under her breath.

Eighteen

We take the expressway to Gladwyne, a short twenty-minute drive in light Thanksgiving Day traffic. We pass one magnificent house after another before Luke turns onto Monk Road. Stopping at a gated driveway, he punches in a code before the gates swing open. We continue up the long drive and arrive at an enormous stone house. The landscaping is meticulous, even in November. Luke pulls into a circular drive leading to the front door and parks. There are several other cars as well, but I don't see a garage. I'm guessing that is around the side or in back.

"You grew up here?" I ask.

Luke glances briefly at the house. "Yes."

"Do you think they will like me?" I ask, nervous. I don't know Luke that well yet. I haven't met anyone in his life except Gina. And technically, I haven't met Gina. I don't think her disparaging me across the counter at Grind Me counts as meeting. I asked about her once and Luke responded she was no one important. I believe him. After all, I'm here with him today, not her.

Luke parks the car before placing his arm across my seat back and meeting my eyes. "My family is…" He pauses here, his eyes moving from mine to the house while he thinks. "My family tends to be difficult."

He slides out of the car after that and is opening my door before I realize he didn't answer my question. Placing a hand on my back as we walk, he guides me towards the door. I'm wondering who else will be here and I wish I'd thought to ask on the drive over.

Thankfully Jean and Everly persuaded me to dress for this. If I'd gone home with Jeannie for Thanksgiving as planned I'd have worn jeans and a sweatshirt. I've ended up playing it safe with a basic black dress and matching heels. From what I can see under Luke's coat he's wearing black slacks and a white button-down dress shirt. I'm so glad I'm not in jeans.

We stop on the stone front porch as Luke rings the doorbell. It's never occurred to me that anyone would ring the doorbell of their childhood home. I try to imagine doing this at my grandparents' house but I can't. Then I remember their home—my home—on Cowbell Lane isn't ours anymore. Will I ring the doorbell when I visit them in Florida?

It feels like everything is changing. My grandparents have moved and I'll be graduating and moving out of student housing in less than six months. Jean will move in with Jonathan after we graduate. Everly will either beat Professor Camden into submission or move to New York. I'll get an apartment somewhere in Philadelphia. Beside me Luke takes my hand and I have to wonder what role he'll play in my life in six months, if any.

The oversized front door swings open and a tall older woman greets us. "Lucas! Welcome home." This woman exudes warmth and hospitality. She doesn't seem difficult as Luke called his family moments ago.

"Mrs. Estes," Luke greets her before introducing me. "This is Sophie. Sophie, Mrs. Estes is our house manager."

House manager? What in the heck is a house manager? I smile and shake her hand before Luke helps me out of my coat and hands both my coat and his to Mrs. Estes. I guess house managers hang up coats? I'm in so over my head.

"Who's here?" Luke inquires.

"Your sister and her husband, your aunt and uncle and the Holletts are all in the living room." She smiles and holds her arm out towards the entry hall, indicating we should head in. She's a tall, trim woman with dark curly hair securely pulled back to the nape of her neck. She's wearing a very expensive-looking tan suit and black pumps. I guess house managers don't wear business casual.

The foyer empties into a grand hallway that appears to be the central point of the house. There's a magnificent stairway leading to the second story. Clearly no expense was spared on finishing details here. I spy an exquisite dining room to my left, a quick glance telling me the Millers could easily seat sixteen for dinner if they chose to.

We pass the dining room in favor of a formal living room. As we pass the threshold he murmurs, "We don't have to stay long." I'm not sure what to make of that. Why are we here if he's already planning our exit?

"Luke!" A stunning woman with hair the same chocolate-brown shade as his rushes over to envelope Luke in a hug. "Mother said you were bringing someone," she says as she turns to me, grinning.

I smile and start to introduce myself but she's hugging me before I have the chance.

"I'm Meredith, Luke's sister," she tells me as she steps back and looks at Luke. "She's a doll. Wherever did you find her?"

Luke and I glance at each other and he smirks at me in a way that causes a spontaneous blush to flood my cheeks.

"This is Sophie," Luke introduces me, ignoring Meredith's question about how we met.

The man Meredith was sitting with when we arrived has walked over to join us and shakes hands with Luke. He's tall like Luke, but leaner. He has a runner's physique and sandy blond hair and is introduced as Meredith's husband Alexander.

"Where's my girl?" Luke asks, looking around the living room. "She's the only reason I show for these things."

"You could at least pretend you care about seeing me, you know." But I can tell Meredith's not mad. This seems to be a running joke between them. "Your niece is napping before dinner." Her smiles fades as she drops her voice. "Mother had the nerve to ask me why I didn't leave her at home with the nanny."

"Remind me why your mother never babysits," Alexander jokes as we proceed into the room while Meredith runs to check on their sleeping daughter.

Luke introduces me to his father, who I learn is a doctor only when he's introduced as, "My father, Dr. Miller." He's sitting near the front of the room with Luke's aunt and uncle, whom I'm also introduced to.

"Lucas, darling, I'm so glad you could make it." A tiny

woman who looks like she could be Meredith's sister approaches us.

Luke leans down and kisses her offered cheek. No hug. "Mother, this is my girlfriend, Sophie Tisdale," he says as he puts an arm around my waist.

Girlfriend? Unless I missed it, he did not introduce me to his father as his girlfriend, just Sophie.

"I told you I was bringing her."

"Yes, I'm so glad your friend could join us." She smiles the least genuine smile imaginable and shakes my hand. "I'm Mrs. Miller. Lovely to meet you."

Upon closer inspection I can see she's not as young as Meredith, obviously. She's definitely had work done though.

She turns back to Luke. "The Holletts have joined us with their lovely daughter Kara. Come say hello." We follow her to a seating arrangement in front of a sizable fireplace lit with a roaring fire.

Mr. and Mrs. Hollett are seated on a sofa with their daughter Kara. Mrs. Miller sits on the adjoining love seat, leaving Luke and I to sit in high-backed chairs. Mrs. Estes stops by to offer us drinks. This is the most formal, uncomfortable holiday ever and it's only just started.

"Kara has just moved back to Philadelphia from Los Angeles." Mrs. Hollett beams with pride. "She was just promoted to a director-level position here in Philadelphia." Mrs. Hollett talks for a bit about Kara's accomplishments in the world of charitable fundraising with Mrs. Miller agreeing to every word.

"Lucas, Kara is looking for a place to buy in the Rittenhouse Square area. Perhaps you can help her locate something suitable." Mrs. Miller beams, her eyes bouncing between Luke and Kara as if she's just come up with this idea. Is his mother trying to set him up with another woman right in front of me?

Kara glances at me briefly, looking mortified, before returning her attention to Luke's mother. "Mrs. Miller, that's such a kind idea, but I have a very qualified realtor."

"Well then, Lucas must take you to dinner soon so you two can catch up." Mrs. Miller smiles indulgently.

Wow. I'd be speechless if anyone was actually speaking to me. She really is trying to set Luke up on a date right in front of me. I glance at Luke. He's got a tumbler of water casually hanging from one hand while his other taps against the armrest. He looks completely relaxed, leaning back in the chair with his leg crossed, one foot resting on the opposite knee.

"Sure, Sophie and I would be happy to have dinner with Kara, Mother. We'll arrange something soon."

Kara shoots me another apologetic look. Luke never looks in my direction at all. I'm so confused. I'm excited he shot his mother down by including me in the theoretical plans, but this feels off. Why did he bring me to this train wreck?

"Oh, I think Sophie would be bored, don't you, Lucas?"

Luke sets his glass down with a thud that makes me jump. "Mother," he begins before being interrupted by a screech as a blur of pink tulle flies past.

"Uncle Luke!" A tiny girl wearing a pink party dress and sweet pink ballet flats launches herself onto Luke's lap. Her dark blonde hair is pulled into a ballerina bun and her tiny fingernails are coated in a sparkly pink polish. I'm already a little bit in love with her.

"Meredith, can you control her, please?" Mrs. Miller's perfect composure looks close to snapping.

"Bella, I think we're having too much fun for your grandmother." Luke stresses the word grandmother and I swear Mrs. Miller's botoxed mouth twitches.

Luke stands with Bella hanging from his neck and holds out a hand, gesturing for me to follow. Bella peers at me over Luke's shoulder as we head out of the living room. Her green eyes sparkle when she spots me. "Hi! I'm Bella! What's your name?"

"I'm Sophie." I smile back at her.

"Are you my family or are you my friend?" she asks me.

"Sophie is my friend," Luke interjects, responding for me. He kisses the top of her head and, turning his head, winks at me.

I'm fairly sure I ovulate right then and there.

We walk through the entry hall of the house and Luke asks Bella if she brought any toys to play with. She wiggles out of his hold and sprints down the hall with Luke and I following. We end up in a casual living area on the opposite side of the house with a view of the back yard. I can see a pool closed up for the season surrounded by more immaculate landscaping with a wooded area beyond that.

There's a TV in this room and a big sectional couch. Huge wooden beams cross the vaulted ceiling. It's almost cozy in here. There's a few toys strewn about and a pink blankie on top of the couch. I assume this was where Bella was napping when we arrived. Bella runs to the other side of the couch and scoops something off the floor.

"Found her!" She beams and cradles the toy to her chest as she walks it back to us. "This is my baby. Her name is Lili. You hold her?" This is directed at me.

"I'd love to hold her, Bella, thank you."

"You have to sit down," she tells me. "You can't hold the baby if you're standing."

I sit on the couch and cuddle the baby doll while Bella hovers over me, tucking a blanket around the doll and offering me her bottle so I can feed her. She offers a lot of tips about how I should handle the baby and I'm wondering if Luke's sister is having another when Bella climbs up on the couch next to me and wraps her arm around mine and snuggles close. I'm about to melt, that is how sweet she is being, when she pats my tummy with her tiny hand and asks me if I have a baby inside my tummy.

"No."

That came from Luke. If there's a way to say the word no that is more unyielding than the way Luke just uttered the one syllable I've never heard it. He pinches the bridge of his nose and addresses Bella.

"Bella Love Halliday, you are not to ask women if they have babies in their stomach. Do you understand me?"

"Mommy does." Bella giggles. "It's a see rat."

"What?" Luke is staring at both of us like we've lost our minds. I'm not sure what I've done, and Bella is three so I think Luke's the one who might need to reassess.

"It's a see rat! Mommy is having a see rat!"

"I think Bella means it's a secret." I look at Luke. For a guy who's as in love with his niece as he clearly is he could use a toddler dictionary.

"Yes! One of those! That is what Mommy is having. I no tell anyone," she adds, shaking her head.

"Have you been practicing being a big sister with Lili?" I ask her, indicating the doll.

"Yes!" Bella is ecstatic that I understand the connection. "I pray ice with Lili!"

Mrs. Estes stops in then to tell us dinner is ready. Luke scoops Bella up and we go ahead to the dining room to find Meredith sliding a chair into the table next to her husband and placing a Disney sippy cup on the table.

"Really, Mother? You thought a three-year-old would eat Thanksgiving dinner alone in the kitchen?"

Mrs. Miller has no reaction to that other than to respond, "No, I thought she'd eat dinner at home with her nanny, but you gave her the day off."

"We gave her the week off, actually," Alexander interjects from his seat to Mrs. Miller's left. "We enjoy spending time with Bella."

Luke places Bella on the seat between her parents before escorting me to the other side of the table and pulling out a chair for me between him and his dad, who is seated at the opposite end of the table from his mom.

I notice Mrs. Miller's seating arrangement has Luke sitting between me and Kara. Our side of the table is me, Luke, Kara, Mrs. Hollett and Mr. Hollett. Across from me is Luke's aunt, then his uncle, Meredith, Bella and Alexander. I look longingly towards Meredith's end of the table, wishing I was closer to friendly faces. Then again, I'm about as far as I can get from Mrs. Miller so I'll take what I can get.

"Lucas, how are things at Baldwin?" The elder Dr.

Miller ignores me completely and starts questioning Luke about the hospital. "I saw Dr. Tan last week at a conference. She said your department profits are the talk of the hospital."

Luke's face is expressionless, but his jaw is doing that tick thing he does when he's annoyed.

They go back and forth with this oddly polite bickering until the food is placed before us. Placed, on individual plates, like in a restaurant. No carved-up turkey or casserole dish of sweet potatoes covered in mini-marshmallows on this table. I wonder what Mrs. Miller would do if I wiped my plate clean of mashed potatoes and asked for more. I have to suppress a giggle, that's how ridiculous the thought of asking Mrs. Miller for seconds is.

The plates are set in front of us with precision by a woman in a chef's uniform. Luke murmurs, "Thank you, Heidi," as she places a plate in front of him, so I gather that the Millers have a full-time chef on staff as well as the house manager.

I wonder if it was Mrs. Miller or Heidi who taught Luke how to make his first peanut butter and jelly sandwich? Wait, why am I even asking myself? Clearly it was Heidi.

Dr. Miller turns his attention to his brother and sister-in-law and I breathe a sigh of relief. My hands are folded in my lap while everyone is being served. Luke reaches under the table and briefly squeezes my hand before picking up his knife and fork. I glance at him and smile as I pick up my utensils as well. I'd have preferred takeout and Luke's couch over this experience, but this is... okay. It's interesting learning more about Luke if nothing else. I relax and take a bite of turkey. Heidi is a whiz, this is delicious.

"Lucas, have you seen Gina? I heard she's back in Philadelphia," Mrs. Miller says.

Gina? Mrs. Miller knows the redheaded troll? Of course she does.

"I have and she is," Luke replies with a finality that indicates he's done discussing the topic.

Crap. I want to know more about Gina! But I don't want to ask Luke about her directly, obviously.

Mrs. Miller takes a sip of wine. "It's a shame things didn't work out between you two."

I knew it! I knew those two were together. My moment of smugness fades. *Be an adult, Sophie*, I chastise myself. *You can't date an older man and expect him not to have a history.* Besides, he's really good in bed and I am enjoying the benefits of that. Wait, he practiced with her. *Stop thinking about Gina and Luke in bed together!*

"I was surprised when your engagement ended. You seemed so well suited." Mrs. Miller's eyes flicker over me.

Wow, that stung. My heart races at the snub and my cheeks flush in embarrassment.

"That engagement ended six years ago, Mother, I think you've had sufficient time to get past your surprise."

Six years ago? Six years ago Luke was engaged and I was in high school. I sit on that thought for a moment. Engaged. What did Luke tell me about her? That she was no one important? Yet he was having dinner with her a month ago, and he was with her again when he walked into Grind Me the following week.

"I heard she just took a position running the

cardiovascular department at Baldwin Memorial," Luke's father interjects.

"She did, yes." Luke spears a piece of turkey with his fork.

"She was a highly sought-after candidate. Well-regarded."

"She's a very talented surgeon," Luke agrees noncommittally.

I feel so stupid. They work at the same hospital? Is he still with her? She's clearly not "no one" as he indicated to me weeks ago. She was his fiancée at one time. And I'm just a college student. I don't even have a job lined up after graduation.

On that note, as if he's just remembering I'm at the table, Luke's father glances at me and asks if I'm a part of the high-school volunteer program at Luke's hospital.

I'm defeated. These people are awful.

"That's enough," Luke begins to reply before I have to, but he's cut off by Bella. She's been quiet throughout most of the meal, but she chooses this moment to stand on her chair and boom, "I'm having a bay bee!" Then she claps her hands excitedly and jumps up and down on her chair.

I knew I liked that kid. The tension is broken and the attention is now on Meredith.

Heidi clears our plates and offers coffee. She's serving tiny individual pumpkin pies as Luke's phone rings and he excuses himself from the table.

I feel a jolt of panic at being left alone with these people without him, but Kara engages me in conversation now that we can see each other without Luke between us. She's very sweet and I enjoy chatting with her. I don't think she had a clue that her mom and Mrs. Miller were planning to set her up with Luke today.

The pies are served and coffee is poured and Luke is still not back. Everyone continues on without him, and it reminds me of Gina at the restaurant weeks ago. I was right about her being used to the frequent interruptions that accompany time spent with Luke. Though now I realize she can probably relate since she is a doctor herself.

I swirl my fork through the whipped-cream dollop on top of my pie. I love pumpkin pie, but I'm not hungry and I'm a little melancholy anyway. I'm a bit shell-shocked from this day.

Heidi clears the dessert plates and announces there is fresh coffee in the living room. Luke meets us there, finishing his call as he walks into the room. He stops briefly to say something to Alexander before heading over to me, apologizing and stating there's an emergency at the hospital he needs to attend to. No objection here.

Mrs. Estes meets us by the door with our coats. Meredith follows us with Bella on her hip. "Luke, do you need me to drive Sophie home so you can get to the hospital?" She smiles and Bella waves at me. "I'd love more time to chat with Sophie." She grins mischievously at Luke.

"Sophie not have a baby in her tummy," Bella adds helpfully and shakes her head.

Meredith's eyes widen. "Bella!" She shoots me an apologetic look. "I'm so sorry. Stupid parenting books advised to be as honest with her as possible. I wish I had lied and told her a gnome would be dropping the baby off like I wanted to."

"It's fine." I wave off her apology.

"Thank you for the altruistic offer, Meredith, but I'm going to send Sophie home in my car and have Alexander drop me at the hospital."

Meredith pouts. "You just don't want me to have any time alone with Sophie."

"You're correct." He smiles at her. "Besides, you can use the time working on manners with my niece," he tells her as he ushers me through the front door.

Nineteen

"You drive, right?" Luke asks as he walks me to his car and opens the driver's side door for me.

"Of course."

"Great." He reaches past me and pushes a button and the car roars to life. He drops the keys onto the center console before tapping the built-in GPS screen. "I'll grab a cab from the hospital when I'm done," he tells me as he buckles me into the seat and presses a button, sliding the seat forward to accommodate my shorter height.

"I'm sorry, Sophie," he says and then he's gone, walking back towards the front door where Alexander is waiting. I'm left alone with a car that I suspect costs more than my college education.

I put it into drive and the GPS immediately encourages me to turn right at the end of the driveway. I'm not even sure if I'm headed to my dorm or Luke's condo, but the car seems to know.

The gates swing open automatically as I near them and I turn onto Monk Road. I'm numb as I drive, replaying the day. Was that as horrible as I think it was? I want to call Jeannie or Everly but I have no idea how to operate the hands-free phone system in this car.

Why did he invite me today? His mother is a

nightmare. Was I just a distraction to foil her setup attempt? The only person he introduced me to as his girlfriend was his mother.

Learning Gina is his ex-fiancée makes me uncomfortable, like he lied to me. Did he? Kind of. She's way more than the no one he indicated she was, but was it my business at the time I asked? Whatever, I'm still pissed.

That was the saddest Thanksgiving ever.

The GPS is directing me to his condo. I tap my thumbs on the steering wheel as I drive and I get progressively more pissed off as the miles pass. The garage door at 10 Rittenhouse Square opens automatically as I pull up. I assume this fancy car has a sensor to match his fancy condo. I park in Luke's spot and think.

What am I supposed to do now? Did Luke indicate if he'd see me later? I have his keys. Did he send me home with his car to wait for him? Am I supposed to let myself into his place or did he just want me out of his parents' house?

I'm over this day. I lock the car and take the elevator to the lobby. I know there's a concierge, I've seen him when we've walked through the lobby to the adjoining Italian restaurant Serafina. It occurs to me now how convenient it is for Luke to take me out to dinner at a restaurant in the lobby of his condo. We go from dinner to fucking without ever leaving the building.

My heels click across the empty marble lobby. It's so quiet, everyone has somewhere to be for the holiday. I set the keys on the counter in front of the concierge, a well-dressed man I estimate to be in his forties.

"Would you see that these get to Dr. Miller?"

"Of course, Miss Tisdale." He's the model of professionalism, impeccable in a gray suit and black tie, not a hair out of place. If he finds it odd that I'm leaving Luke's keys with him he doesn't show it, but maybe this is a common occurrence.

Wait. "How do you know my name?"

"It's my job to know." He offers a polite smile and I wonder how many names he's had to memorize. "Do you need a ride somewhere?"

"No, thank you. I can get a cab out front."

"We have a courtesy town car on site," he says, picking up a phone behind the desk. "I insist."

I'm not going to bicker with him about how I get home so I gracefully accept his offer and head out front, where a black Mercedes is already idling at the curb. The doorman holds the car door open for me so I slide in and give the driver my address.

* * *

Back in my room, I shut the door behind me and lean against it. It's oddly quiet, most everyone gone for the long weekend. Jean won't be back until Sunday. I straighten and check my phone. No messages. I kick off my heels and peel off my nylons before unzipping my dress.

Rummaging through my dresser, I look for something comforting to wear and find a small wrapped package on top of my flannel pajama bottoms. I slip the pants on with an old Penn tee shirt and sit on the edge of my bed with the package.

I tear off the wrapping paper and find a pair of brown

socks. Huh, kind of boring. Then they unravel and I laugh for the first time all day. They're turkey socks. Toe socks, kind of like gloves for your feet. Each toe is a different color and there's a big silly turkey face on the top and gobble-gobble printed around the top.

I love them, and I love that Jean left me a little surprise just when I needed it most. I smile as I text Jean a thank you before crawling under the covers with a textbook.

* * *

A knock on the door wakes me. It's dark outside but my room is ablaze in light. I fell asleep studying with the lights on and now I'm disoriented. The knock sounds again as I walk over and swing the door open. Luke is filling my entire doorway, leaning one arm against the frame.

"How did you get in here?" I'm confused. You can't just walk into the building, even if you're a student.

He takes me in for a moment then places his hands on my hips, backs me into the room and shoves the door closed with his foot. Then his mouth is on mine like he's starving for me and I gasp when he wraps a hand in my hair and tugs, angling my head exactly how he wants it.

"Why did you leave?" He stops kissing me and stares at me, waiting for an answer.

I pull away from him and put some space between us. "How did you get in here?" I repeat.

"Did you not want me here?"

"Stop!" I'm louder than I meant to be and I lower my voice. "Just stop it with your non-answers."

He crosses his arms across his chest and rubs his bottom lip with his thumb. Which is annoying, because it always does things to me and I'm trying to focus. "A blonde girl named Paige told security I was with her and brought me up." He drops his arms and stuffs his hands into his pockets. He's wearing the same thing I saw him in earlier, but he looks wrinkled now, tired. "You weren't answering your phone," he adds. "Are you ignoring me?"

"I fell asleep," I say, picking up the phone and glancing at it. "I forgot to turn the mute off when I left your parents' house."

"You put it on mute to meet my family?" he asks with a tiny smirk.

"I wanted to make a good impression," I reply, then sag as I recall the day.

"You did," he assures me. "You did make a good impression."

I look at him in disbelief. "They hated me. Your mother tried to set you up on a date while I was sitting right next to you."

"You made a good impression with me," he clarifies. "And that's all that matters."

My eyes burn then. Tears form and I fight them off. "Those people are awful, Luke." My voice catches. "Who raised you?"

He closes the distance between us and wraps me up in his arms, my head resting under his chin. He kisses the top of my head as he says, "A lovely British woman named June."

I laugh. "Really?"

"Of course. You don't think my parents got their hands dirty, do you?"

"No," I sigh and bury my face in his chest. He still smells of aftershave and faintly like hospital disinfectant, but I like it. "I was too upset to eat the pumpkin pie."

"I'll buy you all the pumpkins in Philadelphia and we'll make our own." He runs his hands up and down my back. "I'm sorry, Sophie, I shouldn't have brought you there."

What? "You didn't want me to meet them?"

"I wanted you there for myself, Sophie, because you make everything better. It was selfish of me to bring you." His hands slide under my flannel pajama bottoms and cup my ass. "I should have ordered takeout and kept you naked in my condo all day persuading you to let me fuck this perfect ass."

I shove him away. He looks surprised for a second until I say, "Gina."

His expression closes, giving me nothing. "Gina is a non-issue, Sophie."

"You were engaged to her!" I'm outraged. How can he be so dismissive of his relationship to her and my feelings about it? Will I be nobody to him someday too?

"A long time ago."

"I was in high school."

He looks confused for a moment then asks, "When I was engaged to Gina?"

"Yes," I reply, but I don't meet his eyes.

"That bothers you? That I was engaged or that you were in high school when I was engaged?"

"Both. Neither. I don't know."

I'm staring at my toes as Luke tips my chin up to look into my eyes. "I'm a lot older than you, Sophie. Is it an issue or not?"

"It's not." I shake my head. "Unless I'm thinking about her." I stress the last word.

"She's hardly the only woman I've…" He stops when I glare at him and laughs.

"Why is she still around?" I sound like a crazy person. He can't be friends with his ex? But she was a bitch to me, wasn't she? "Never mind."

"We have business together, that's all, Sophie. She's no one to me." He says that last part with his lips hovering over my ear and his breath tickles me, making me shiver. He cups the back of my neck and runs his thumb over my earlobe. I nod and then wrap my arms around his neck as I kiss him.

"I kinda love imagining high-school you not putting out," he says when I break the kiss. He glances around my tiny dorm room with interest. His eyes move over what is obviously Jean's side of the room and stop on my side. Our room is small and messy. My dorm may not be far from Luke's Rittenhouse Square condo physically, but it's a world away financially. My room is quite literally the size of his walk-in closet.

He steps over a foot and examines my corkboard. God, what do I have on there? The bra I wore today is hanging over my desk chair. He fingers it as he peruses the top of my desk, a messy assortment of textbooks and notes. He's probably wondering what he's doing with a college student. Fuck, are those panties on the floor next to his toe?

I'm not sure what to say as he continues looking his fill. I'm not going to apologize for my room. I might be a little embarrassed, but I'm not apologizing. He lived in a dorm room once too, I'm sure. A long time ago. Damn it.

Is that what he's thinking about? How long it's been since he was a student? How different we are?

He turns to me with a sly grin. "You've never had sex in here."

Obviously I haven't. He's the only person I've had sex with and that's all been at his place. "No."

"We can rectify that now." He grins.

Oh, that's what was on this mind? He wants to be the one to fuck me in my dorm room? "Yes, please."

"Yes, please?" he repeats back to me. "So polite, you little hussy," he says as he covers the three steps that separate us. "Should I be polite?" He bends and kisses me under my left ear, not waiting for an answer. "Come on, Sophie, let me make love to you, baby. I'll make it good for you, I swear." He's kissing me along my jaw and keeping his hands chastely on my hips, over my pajamas. I'm not sure what is happening right now. "I'll just put the tip in, okay?"

I laugh. He's giving me clichéd college sex lines.

"I'll still respect you in the morning, baby."

I'm laughing when he covers my mouth with his. He keeps whispering ridiculous lines to me, but his mouth and hands are their usual Luke perfection. I play along because it's funny, but it's hot too. Also, I love it when he loses focus and smirks at something I've said. He takes his time, probably more time than he's ever needed to take.

"Can I take off your shirt?" he asks, as if there's a possibility I might say no.

Jesus, yes! I want to scream at him. He's got me so worked up and we've still got all our clothes on. Heavy petting is bullshit when you've already ridden the bull. I unbutton his pants and ask for permission to "touch it." This earns me a laugh and I think I might have him then, ready to end this game and pound the fuck out of me on my twin-sized bed, but no. He regains composure and guides my hand up and down the length of him.

"I want you to be my first, Luke. I know you'll make it good." I am laying it on now. "I've wanted you inside of me since the first time I saw you." It's getting harder to speak with his hands down my pants. "Your fingers, God knows how I loved watching them as you brought your coffee cup to your perfect lips. I'd go home after my shift and lie in this bed and touch myself while thinking about you. Before the clinic, before I even knew your name, I'd lie right here thinking about you while making myself come."

"Fuck!" Luke roars. He's so loud in the quiet room it startles me for a second before he's ripping my flannel pajama pants down my legs and lowering his own. He doesn't even get his pants all the way down before he's inside of me.

He strokes back and forth, so deep, kissing me long and hard while he's burrowed within me, before pulling back enough to watch himself slide in and out of my body.

"I won't come in you, Sophie."

It takes me a moment to realize he never put on a condom. I'm not sure if we're still roleplaying or not, but I trust him enough not to worry about it further. I'm on the pill, which I take every day faithfully.

He gives up watching to drive into me. He's still got his feet on the floor and my back is on the bed with my pelvis raised, legs over his shoulders. He pounds into me, our skin slapping in the quiet room, my moans as quiet as I am able to keep them.

He changes the angle and presses down on my clit with his thumb and I come all over his cock. He pulls out and orders me on my knees. "On the floor, now. You're going to suck my cock and swallow." He has to help me off the bed, my body a wet noodle after that orgasm, but I obey and sink to my knees before him. He slides into my mouth the moment my knees hit the floor.

"Taste yourself, Sophie. You just came all over me and now you're gonna swallow my come."

I moan around his dick and he asks me if I like it. The insides of my thighs are slick and his words are making me wetter.

He grabs the side of my face and fucks my mouth. No gentle teasing now, he just takes. His hands are knotted in my hair when he comes and it's easy to swallow it all at this angle, most of it bypassing my tongue and going straight down the back of my throat.

He picks me up off the floor when I'm done and lays me on top of him in my small bed while our heart rates decrease. "You filthy bitch." He slaps my ass as I lie on top of him, running my nails lightly across his chest.

"What?" I'm so tired. Why is he still talking? "What did I do?"

"You masturbated while thinking about me, apparently."

"Oh my God." I stop running my nails across his chest so I can hide my face in my hands. "I didn't mean to tell you that. You had me all worked up. Just... forget I said that."

His chest shakes as he laughs at me. "Not a chance."

Twenty

I slide the pie into Luke's high-end Miele stainless-steel oven and search for a timer.

"How long?" Luke walks up behind me and presses my body into the oven, his front to my back. My hair is up in a bun while I bake, leaving my neck wide open, which he takes advantage of with his mouth. I lean into his touch, desire warming my skin.

"Forty-five minutes," I tell him and he punches the time into a digital panel on the stove before turning me to face him.

"You smell like nutmeg."

"Does that turn you on, Dr. Miller?"

He laughs. "Everything about you turns me on, Miss Tisdale." He's walking me backwards, hands on my waist until my butt hits the kitchen island before he picks me up and sits me on the counter. He spreads my legs and stands between them, then pins me in place by placing his hands on either side of me on the granite countertop.

"Sophie." He touches his forehead to mine then tilts his head and kisses me briefly before stepping back. "We need to talk."

What? My eyes fly to his and my heart races as I try to piece together what he wants to talk about. I thought we resolved everything yesterday at my dorm. After the awful day at his parents and the incredible dorm sex that followed, he told me to grab enough stuff for the weekend and took me back to his condo.

We went out this morning hand in hand for coffee and bagels before hitting the grocery story for pumpkin pie ingredients. Luke mentioned the store had pies already prepared, but quickly shut up at the look on my face.

Now he leans against the counter across from me and sighs, running a hand over his face before crossing his arms across his chest and looking at my feet dangling off his countertop. "What the hell are on your feet?"

"Turkey socks," I reply, wiggling my toes.

He shakes his head in response. Yeah, I don't think my socks are what he wants to talk about. What is it? Have I trashed his kitchen? Is he some kind of obsessive-compulsive about to flip out over dirty mixing bowls?

"Yesterday in your dorm room," he begins, slowly. I stare at him waiting, wanting him to spit it out already, but I sit silently, waiting for him to continue.

"I shouldn't have done that," he finishes.

Done what? The kinky roleplaying? I thought that was fun. Wait, did I initiate that or did he? Does he think I'm a freak? Or does he mean he shouldn't have come to my dorm at all?

"I shouldn't have..." He pauses, searching for how he wants to phrase this, and all I can do is stare at him and wait. "Entered you without a condom."

Oh. Okay. He's right, I guess. I want to tell him it's fine, no big deal, but I tread carefully, because I liked it. I liked that he lost control enough to want to. I liked that he'd trusted me enough to. And I damn well liked the feeling of him, sliding inside of me, knowing it was impossible to get any closer to him than that. Then when he came down my throat telling me to taste myself on him? I get a little wet remembering it and I shift on the countertop.

I want to tell him these things and remind him I'm on the pill and that he didn't come inside of me, but... gynecologist. I really want to avoid a safe-sex lecture from my lover.

"I'm taking the pill every day." I smile at him, wanting to lighten the mood. "And I don't have any STD's," I add in as a joke.

He doesn't look amused. At all. Instead he tells me to, "Stay," like a child and leaves the kitchen.

What is his problem? I fear he's going to whip out a pregnancy test and make me pee on it in front of him. He walks back into the room with a sheet of paper. Oh, shit. Does he have some kind of STD? Is that what he's so worried about? What the hell is on that paper?

"I had this done in October," he says, handing the sheet to me. I stare at it with no idea what I'm supposed to be looking for.

"Luke, I don't know what any of this means," I say, indicating the sheet. "What are you trying to say?"

"I'm trying to tell you that I'm clean, you have nothing to worry about."

"Great." I smile, relieved.

"No, Sophie. It's not great." He looks annoyed. "You should always have this information prior to having unprotected sex." He runs a hand over his eyes. "I'm setting a really shit example for you. Promise me you'll never allow anyone to touch you without a condom before exchanging test results first."

"You want me to have all my future lovers hand over test results prior to ditching the condoms. Got it, Doctor," I say sarcastically because this conversation stings. I can't look at him right now. I cannot believe he's lecturing me about future lovers. Am I supposed to be touched by his concern? Creeped out by his authoritative decree? Or devastated that he's talking to me about other men touching me?

"Goddamn it." Luke mutters something about going to use the gym as he stalks out of the kitchen. I hear the front door slam two minutes after that and I still haven't moved from where he sat me on the counter.

What just happened? Is he mad at me or I at him?

I clean up the kitchen and take the pie out when the timer dings, then stare out the kitchen windows at the Philadelphia skyline, still confused about what set him off. Was I not taking his safe-sex talk seriously enough? Forgive me, but being lectured by my current lover about future lovers pisses me off.

Luke's still not back from the gym. I know it's in this building, but I'm not sure which floor so I couldn't go find him even if I wanted to. I'm bored, I'd like to go out for a walk and window-shop the cute stores along 18th Street, but I don't have a key to get back in and besides, I don't want to leave without talking to him.

I wander back into the kitchen and use my iPad to look up recipes on Pinterest. Determining Luke has all the necessary ingredients for pumpkin chocolate-chip cookies, I set to work on those to keep busy. This kitchen is a baker's dream. Tons of counter space and a big high-end oven. Plus a dishwasher to help clean it all up. I can't imagine Luke using any of it—I'm not sure why he even has mixing bowls and baking sheets. I don't want to think too hard about it either, because I don't want to imagine some previous girlfriend making herself at home like I am right now.

The front door clicks open a while later, while I'm peering into the oven checking on the two trays of cookies inside. Heels click-clack a second before a female voice calls out for Luke.

I shut the oven door.

"Luke, darling, where are you?" She sounds like she's crying. There's a strange crying woman in Luke's apartment? How did she get in? I step into the hallway but I don't see anyone. A moment later her heels click from the hallway that leads past the coat closet to the master bedroom, as if she's just checked the bedroom looking for Luke. Interesting. The heels click-clack towards me and then Gina rounds the corner and stops facing me.

She's dabbing at her eyes with a tissue, her face distraught, until she sees me. A flash of surprise crosses her face, but she quickly regains herself.

"Where is Luke?" she asks me, still sniffing into her tissue, tears welled up in her eyes. She looks down the hall that leads to his office as if she's about to walk past me in search of him.

Bitch.

I take in her appearance. Her hair and makeup are perfect, her clothing impeccable. It's the day after Thanksgiving, most of America is in jeans or sweatpants and this woman is wearing four-inch heels, a pencil skirt and a blouse neatly tucked in with a slim belt around her waist. A camel-colored wool coat is folded over her arm, as if she took it off in the elevator on the way up, planning on staying awhile.

"He's…" I'm about to tell her he's at the gym but she probably knows exactly which floor the gym is on. She managed to get past the front desk and into the condo just fine. In a moment of bitchiness I respond, "He's not here."

Her tears dry up in an instant. "Where is he?" she asks as she eyes me, standing in Luke's foyer in jeans and a sweater. My shoes are off, my hair up. I'm clearly comfortable in Luke's home, but then again, so is she. She walked right in the front door seeming to know exactly where to look for Luke in this giant place.

I'm saved from answering as the timer sounds on the oven. "He's not here," I repeat as I turn and head into the kitchen, hoping she will take the hint and see herself out the same way she saw herself in. "I'll tell him you stopped by," I add while silently begging her to get out.

I don't hear anything for a moment, then as I silence the oven timer she click-clacks… into the kitchen. I ignore her as I slide an oven mitt over my hand and remove the trays from the oven, placing them on the burners to cool.

"You're making cookies? And a pie?" She bursts out laughing, wiping away tears from the corners of her eyes. "Adorable. Are you doing arts and crafts too?" She looks around the kitchen as if she expects to see macaroni art in progress.

I'm not a fighter, so I remain quiet. There's really no response to that anyway. Jean would have put Gina in her place with a few well-said words. Everly would have jumped on her monkey-style and started ripping her hair out. I smirk a little at the thought, but I keep my mouth shut as I move the cookies to a cooling rack.

"So where's Luke?"

I don't feel like answering her. It's not normally in my nature to be unhelpful, but Gina brings out my inner bitch. "He's out." I look up at her and smile, trying my best to appear like she's not bothering me.

Gina eyes me for a moment before responding. "You don't know where he is, do you?" She seems smug. I'm not sure if she's smug thinking I don't know, or smug because she thinks by taunting me I'm going to answer her. I just smile and scoop balls of cookie dough onto the baking pans I just emptied.

"Aren't you going to offer me a coffee? That is what you do for a living, isn't it, Sophie?" Gina smiles at me. Evil. Bitch.

I look at her and flick my eyes to the Keurig on the counter. "You operate on hearts for a living, I'm sure you can figure out a single-serve coffeemaker."

"Luke's slumming it with a barista who won't even make coffee without being paid." She laughs. "You're cute, Sophie. I hope you're enjoying this time playing kinky Betty Crocker with Luke because it's not going to last. This infatuation he has with you will not last. You think a Miller marries a barista? It's never going to happen, sweetheart."

Marry? Wow. I've been with Luke for a month. No one is talking marriage, but Gina is threatened, that's for sure. I don't know why though. They broke up years ago based on what Luke said at Thanksgiving.

"And you think he wants you back?" I raise an eyebrow in her direction and place a sweet smile on my face.

She doesn't answer, instead runs her hands across the granite countertop and surveys the kitchen. "I think Luke is at a settling-down age and we have a history together. I'm a suitable match for him," she adds, stressing the last part.

I wish I knew who broke up with whom. I have no idea why things ended between them. As it is, I can't say much without revealing that I know nothing.

"Plus his hands." Gina sighs. "He's very good with his hands, isn't he? I bet he's a huge improvement over the boys you normally fuck. A little word of advice, Sophie, commit it to memory because Luke's a hard act to follow in bed."

My chest tightens and I feel both rage and fear. Rage that she's reminiscing about having sex with Luke right in front of me and fear for the same reasons. I'm not a confrontational girl and she's making me feel like I'm under attack. No, I *am* under attack.

"Has he taken you shopping yet for the gala?" She eyes me up and down. "I assume he's bringing you?"

I drop a ball of cookie dough onto the baking sheet. I don't know anything about a gala, but I know she's looking for a reaction.

"I was planning on wearing a dress from Target." I smile. "From last season's clearance rack, obviously."

"You probably would, wouldn't you?" She snorts. "I cannot wait to look back on this and laugh. When Luke and I are back together and you're nothing but a bad memory."

I cannot believe Luke was engaged to this person. She is nothing like me. What did he see in her? What does he see in me? My insecurities about being nothing more than a fuck toy for a rich man resurface. I'm graduating in a few months with a degree in corporate accounting. If I'm lucky I'll get a job offer from a mid-sized corporation. If I'm not lucky I'll be working in a strip mall preparing tax refunds.

In other words, not a heart surgeon.

The front door opens and Gina tosses me a smug look before rushing into the hall. "Luke!" Her voice is distraught and I can already hear the tears in her voice. I wonder if she double-majored in drama and pre-med.

"Where is Sophie?" Luke asks, and I clearly hear her reply about what a darling I am, inviting her in for coffee while she waited and keeping her distracted with stories from Thanksgiving.

Bitch. I cringe at the picture she just painted. I slide the last of the cookies into the oven as the door to Luke's office closes. So he's going to entertain her and listen to her fake tears. Gross.

I clean up the kitchen for the second time today and watch the oven timer. Nine minutes. Five minutes. Two minutes. The timer dings and I remove the last tray from the oven and transfer the cookies to a plate to cool before placing the cookie sheets in the dishwasher.

They're still in his office. I consider trying to eavesdrop from the adjoining room, I really do. But that's not my style, and truthfully Gina does not interest me enough to sneak around.

I grab my iPad off the counter with one hand and a cookie with the other and cut through the dining room to the great room. Luke never uses this room. He hasn't even fucked me in this room. I smile thinking about that, since we've made use of most of the condo. I love the views of Philadelphia from here and peering down on the treetops of Rittenhouse Square Park below.

The room itself is mammoth with two seating areas. I can't imagine Luke picking out sofas or lamps. I wonder if whoever stocked the kitchen with bakeware decorated this room, but quickly discount that idea. This room was professionally decorated. The entire condo was, minus those three empty bedrooms. I still find their complete emptiness a little odd. I imagine the decorator cried at not being able to create guest suites with mounds of fluffy comforters and expensive pillows plumped just so.

While beautiful, this room is not lived in. Looking around, I wonder if Luke's ever put a Christmas tree up in here. I giggle at the thought. There is no way, which is too bad, because there is an empty alcove in this room in front of a huge window with views of the park. I imagine the architect pictured a grand piano in this space, but it's perfect for a Christmas tree.

I sit in one of the armchairs and surf the internet on my iPad before the office door clicks open, finally. Luke tells Gina to call his office on Monday if she needs anything as he walks her to the front door. I'd rather hear him tell her to call him never, but at least she's leaving. I stay put in the chair.

The front door closes and the house is quiet. I know Luke didn't leave with her, but I don't hear him. A few minutes later Luke walks into the room with a handful of cookies.

"You made cookies?" He winks at me as he stuffs one

in his mouth. He's in athletic pants and a short-sleeved tee shirt. His hair is tousled, like he ran a towel through it after his workout. I hate that Gina saw him like this.

"I did," I reply, not sure what to make of him right now. I guess we're not fighting about condoms anymore.

"What are you doing in here?" he asks, inhaling another cookie and glancing around the unused room. "I couldn't find you."

I shrug. "I didn't know what to do with myself while I was waiting for you to finish with your ex-fiancée."

"Miss Tisdale, is that sarcasm I'm hearing?" He leans over me and places his now empty hands on the chair arms, pinning me in place. "I'm very finished with my ex-fiancée, Sophie." He leans in and kisses me lightly on the lips.

"Why is she always around then?" I ask before I can think better of it. I trust Luke. I'm not even going to say it's because I don't trust Gina, because she's irrelevant. She can't make him do anything he doesn't want to do. I simply don't like her, or her intentions, but it's none of my business.

"It's just... work stuff, Sophie," he says, straightening. "I'm going to take a shower. Do you want to go shopping? Gina said something about you wanting to go to Target?"

I laugh then. She's such a bitch. "Yeah, Luke, let's go to Target."

Twenty-One

We do go to Target, and let me tell you, Target with Luke is a lot of fun. I ask him if we can get a tree and he looks a little bewildered by the request but agrees. And when I mention while we look at the pre-lit trees in Target that I've never had a real tree because my grandfather is allergic to them, Luke looks at me for a moment, his gaze moving across my face like he's imagining me as a child, and then pulls out his phone and makes a call. By the time we finish shopping there's a ten-foot balsam fir tree set up and strung with lights in Luke's great room.

He tells me to pick out "whatever trees need," but I refuse, only agreeing to pick the tree decor once he admits that he's partial to blue and that the elf ornaments are funny. Which leads to my discovery that Luke has never seen the movie *Elf*.

While Luke goes to locate a DVD of *Elf* I scour the seasonal department picking all the blue ornaments and elves that I think Luke will like. He comes back with an armful of stuff and dumps it in the cart like a kid with a black American Express card. Then he smacks my ass right in the middle of the aisle and asks what else we can buy at Target.

I laugh and ask how he gets food and paper towels

without ever shopping and he tells me that Mrs. Geiger takes care of all of that. I look at him blankly, having no idea who Mrs. Geiger is, until he informs me that he has a housekeeper who stops in during the week. Apparently she does everything. Shopping, laundry, dry-cleaning runs, cleaning, changing sheets, emptying the dishwasher. Everything. Rich people are weird.

We go back to Luke's with bags of stuff, and looking at the size of his car, it's a good thing he's had a tree delivered. I don't think the engineers at Mercedes had Christmas trees in mind when they built the S63.

Unpacking the bags is even more fun. We carry all the bags into the kitchen and start unloading, but I keep finding things that aren't ornaments.

"You bought red and white striped elf socks?" I ask, holding them up, confused. They're knee-highs.

"Not for me," he replies. "You like funny socks. And pumpkin. You like pumpkin." He pulls a tube of pumpkin spice lip balm out of a bag. He hands it to me and I put it on then tilt my neck back and raise up on my tiptoes to kiss him. Things escalate pretty quickly after that.

My sweater is off before I even realize what is happening. He tosses it on the granite island and then unzips my jeans and yanks both my jeans and panties to mid-thigh before picking me up and sitting my naked ass on the edge of the island countertop.

He slides my bottoms off the rest of the way until they land in a puddle on the floor that he kicks aside before lowering his own pants only enough to pull out his cock. He strokes the length of himself several times while I watch, itching to reach forward and do that for him. He spreads my legs apart and steps between them, hooking my right thigh in the crook of his left elbow, his right hand still stroking himself. He's staring at the slit between my legs, spreading my lips open with his fingers.

My heart is racing and my breathing hitches. I can feel the heat and pressure building and moisture begins to slick my passage. He steps in closer, my thighs spread obscenely wide, my bare bottom on the edge of the counter. I lean back on my hands and watch as Luke places the head of his penis against me. I suck in a breath, not sure I'm wet enough for him just yet. He's so big and he's always had me dripping for him before entering me.

My apprehension is for naught as he doesn't enter me, but instead starts slapping my open pussy with his cock.

"Oh, God." The sight is too much combined with all the blood pumping through me. Every nerve ending is alive with want. I bite my lip and drop to my elbows, looking at the ceiling.

"No." Luke's voice startles me and I move my gaze to his. "You'll watch."

I blink at him and murmur an agreement before he clarifies, "Eyes here, Sophie," indicating where our bodies are connected. His penis is sliding up and down along my spread lips as he coats himself in my wetness.

I can only nod as I pick my elbows off the counter and return to resting my upper body on my hands, the angle perfect for watching. With my full attention where he wants it, Luke grabs himself and guides the head of his penis to my wet, waiting opening. He sticks the tip in, bare, nothing between us. I feel his gaze move from where he's resting just inside of me to my face. I look up and nod before returning my attention to his cock, sliding inside of me one slow inch at a time.

He slides most of the way out then slams back inside of me and I whimper. Not from pain, but from pure pleasure, watching increasing my hedonistic enjoyment. He slips his right arm under my left knee so now I'm splayed open with both legs dangling over his arms, bouncing as he thrusts into me.

It's so good. So, so good. I want to drop my head back in defeat to the pleasure but Luke is insistent, reminding me every time I look away. He's alternating between watching us and watching me.

"I love those noises you make. I think I could come from nothing more than the sound of your voice when I'm fucking you," Luke says above the slapping of our skin and the incoherent noises I'm indeed making. "When you get close you start chanting my name. 'Luke, Luke, Luke.' I almost blow my load early every time, listening to you, knowing you're close. Knowing I did that to you."

"You do, Luke." I'm breathless and so ready. "You always do."

"I'm going to come inside of you, Sophie." He thrusts, yanking my thigh up, changing the angle slightly. "I'm going to come in you so hard my come will be leaking out of you for the rest of the day."

Listening to him describe it while pistoning in and out of my body pushes me over the edge and I come, my orgasm so intense it hurts when he thrusts back in. He stills then for a moment, buried in me balls deep, before I feel him twitch as he moans his own release. It does feel different, warmer, wetter. It feels so intimate. I mean, sex is always intimate, but this is different. It feels like a compliment, if bodily fluids can be described that way.

He leans forward until our lips touch and then I wrap my arms around his neck, pulling him closer while we kiss. He pulls away as he slides out of me. He's still got both of my legs spread open, hooked over his elbows, and he makes no move to drop them, instead focusing on watching his come leak out of me.

"Fuck, that is hot."

I'd be embarrassed, but he is so into it that it just turns me on more. He finally releases one of my legs only to stick two fingers into me, coating them with his release and then moving them to my clit.

"No, no, I can't," I protest. He can't possibly think he's going to make me come again. I'm still pulsating from the last one.

"You can." He drops my other leg now to unsnap my bra and he bends, taking a nipple in his mouth as he works me with his fingers below. Of course he proves himself right, working another orgasm out of me before we're through.

"Luke, you bought *Elf on the Shelf?*" I ask, holding up the box. I'm still sitting on the countertop. Luke just cleaned me up with a paper towel while I about died of embarrassment. It's a lot messier without a condom. I tried to take the paper towel from him and do it myself but he wouldn't allow it.

"I found it by the DVD's," he replies, as if this explains everything. "It's an elf."

This isn't a tradition I did with my grandparents and I can't imagine Luke did either. "I think this is for little kids," I say, reviewing the box.

Luke shrugs and pulls a menu out of the drawer. "Do you want to order in or go down to Serafina?"

"No!" I blurt out. "Not Serafina."

He looks confused. "You don't like Serafina?"

"I love Serafina," I say, then realize I've painted myself in a corner. I don't want to admit I'm feeling weird about Luke always taking me out to eat at a restaurant that's conveniently located in his lobby. I'm behaving like a brat. We just went to Target in public, it's not like he's hiding me.

He looks at me like I'm going to elaborate. When I don't, he puts the menu away and picks my panties up off the floor and slides them up to mid-thigh, then repeats the motions with my jeans before lifting me off the counter and sliding them the remaining way up. He even zips and buttons me back into my jeans and I gotta admit, watching his huge hands dress me makes me want to rip everything off all over again.

"What's your favorite Italian restaurant, Sophie?" he asks as he holds my sweater up for me to put my arms through.

"Lombardi's," I reply automatically.

"Okay," he says and slides his keys off the counter. "We'll go to Lombardi's."

"Luke! Lombardi's is forty-five minutes away in Horsham. And it's not your scene, it's very casual." I feel like such an ass. "Serafina's is fine. Let's just eat downstairs."

He pulls me closer. "You don't think I'm casual?"

"Luke, please," I laugh. "You're the least casual person I know."

"Hmm, maybe," he murmurs into my hair. "I don't

feel casual about you," he says, kissing the top of my head. "So maybe serious isn't all bad."

What is this guy doing to me?

Twenty-Two

"He bought you an Elf on the Shelf?" Everly is staring at me like I've just announced we had a three-way with an elf.

"Yeah. Neither of us really knew what it was, but we looked it up and now he texts me pictures of the elf every morning," I say with a big stupid grin on my face.

"Pictures of the elf on his dick?" Everly asks hopefully.

"No! Pictures of the elf doing funny stuff around his house." Everly is speechless. "Never mind." I wave a hand.

"Holy shit. He's in love with you."

"No." I shake my head. "No, we're just having fun."

It's a week after Thanksgiving and the first I've seen Everly since before the holiday. We were slammed with customers this morning and now it's finally slowed down enough to catch up.

"Wait. Would that be a bad thing? If he loved me?" I ask. She seems kind of appalled.

Everly softens. "Well, no, it's not bad. It's just you're so young."

"I'm the same age as you," I point out.

"No, I know." Everly is treading lightly now, which is

odd for Everly. "You just don't have a lot of experience with men," she says. "Are you ready to commit to something serious?"

"I don't know," I reply as I examine the ends of my hair. "This conversation is silly. We've been together less than two months."

"Do you think this conversation will be easier in a month when you're so far gone in love with him there's no turning back? Will you be happy being with a man who has to run off to the hospital at all hours of the day and night?"

"His hours aren't that bad, really. Most of his practice is scheduled appointments. Unless he's on call at the hospital."

"Yeah, most of his practice involves him looking at other women's pussies. Right now you're the hottest pussy he sees, but how will you feel when you're forty and you know he's seeing twenty-year-old pussy at work?"

"Everly, eww." Of course, now I'm thinking about it.

"And his family is awful," Everly continues. "Think about all that before you tell me you're just having fun."

"He sounds like such a catch when you phrase it that way," I reply sarcastically.

"You're the catch, Sophie. Don't sell yourself short."

"I'm the child of a teenage mother and I don't even know who my father is."

"Your mother has nothing to do with you, Sophie. You made yourself who you are, not her. You're a smart, beautiful girl who will be graduating soon with honors. You're the most caring, responsible person I know."

"Okay, enough about me. Tell me about your

weekend. Did you make any headway with Professor Camden?" I ask her as I pour myself a coffee.

"I…" Everly starts to say, but then stops. Shaking her head, she says, "I don't know what is going on anymore, Sophie."

"What do you mean?" It's so odd to see Everly anything less than confident. "You always know what's going on. You have a plan, remember? Six months till graduation, six months to make Finn Camden fall in love with you," I remind her.

"I know!" She throws her hands up in the air. "I know, I know, but I'm so confused."

"Is everything okay?" I'm concerned. Everly is off her game and that is rare.

"Yeah." She nods, as if to reassure herself. Then she looks past me to the counter. "Your stalker is here again."

I sigh. "Regular customers are not stalkers, Everly. We're a coffee shop. People come in, they get coffee." I walk past her to help the man waiting at the counter and place a big smile on my face, ready to help.

"Sophie." The man says my name and pauses, and that split second is all I need to realize that something is not quite right. Why is this man referring to me by name? I know it's pinned to the front of my apron, but customers rarely use it.

"Could you sit with me for a few minutes?" he asks, gesturing to the empty tables filling Grind Me.

What the heck? I glance sideways at Everly. She's wearing a smug told-you-so expression on her face.

"Um," I reply, unsure how to proceed. "I'm working, but thank you." I give him my best professional smile.

"I can wait until your break," he offers. "Or meet you

after?"

Shit.

I try again. "The thing is, I have a boyfriend. So I don't think I can meet you after my shift." I try my professional smile again. I hope I'm getting it right.

The man smiles in response, but it's not dejected, it's amused. "I'm afraid I might be giving you the wrong impression. I wasn't asking you out."

Oh.

"Besides, I'm far too old for you."

"A little young for her, actually," Everly mutters and the man shoots her a look.

He pulls a wallet from the breast pocket of his coat and opens it, revealing a badge and an ID, which Everly promptly swipes out of his hand. "My name is Boyd Gallagher," he says, still looking at me. He pauses, apparently expecting this to mean something to me.

I shift from foot to foot behind the counter. Am I in some kind of trouble?

"Feds aren't really her fetish, but I know a girl at school who'd be so into you," Everly pipes in, still reviewing the wallet in her hand.

"Everly!" The stranger and I reply at the same time and it breaks the tension a little. I smile as the man retrieves his wallet from Everly's hand and places it back into his pocket.

He sighs and runs a hand through his hair before moving his attention back to me. "Sophie, I'm your brother."

Twenty-Three

"So what did he want?" Luke asks me later that afternoon.

"What did he want?" I repeat, slightly annoyed.

"Yes, Sophie. What did he want?" Luke's voice is clipped. "You wait until today to mention that a man has been hanging out in your coffee shop for over a month watching you work, then today announces that he's your long-lost brother. Why? What does he want?"

"I don't know," I say quietly. I'm lying down on my dorm bed staring at the ceiling and talking to Luke on the phone. "But I have a brother." I breathe into the phone for a moment before continuing. "You have Meredith, Luke. And Alexander and Bella. I've always wanted a sibling, or even a cousin. It would be nice to have someone else in the world besides my grandparents."

"How do you know he's telling you the truth, Sophie?" Luke says. I can hear the hospital buzzing in the background. I know he's busy but he insisted on talking to me after I texted him this bombshell.

"We share the same father," I say, my voice wobbling. "His father"—I pause—"our father, was a US Congressman running for a Senate seat when he met my mother. He was twenty years older than her, and married

165

to Boyd's mother." I'm humiliated recapping this to Luke.

"Go on," Luke encourages.

"My birth certificate lists my father as unknown. My grandparents had no idea who he could have been and my mom refused to name him. She died before I was two, so I never had the chance to ask her myself. She volunteered for Congressman Gallagher's Senate campaign the summer before her freshman year of college."

"Sophie, whatever your parents did twenty years ago has nothing to do with you and the person you are today."

"I guess."

"I know," he counters.

"He had a picture."

"What kind of picture?" Luke asks, with an edge to his voice. I can hear hospital alarms beeping in the background, but Luke doesn't rush me, just waits for my response.

"It was a picture of our dad with my mom. It's the night he was elected Senator, at the campaign headquarters. They're in a room full of people and she's looking at him like she worships him while he's smiling for the camera." I swallow and Luke is quiet, listening. "Boyd was ten when I was born. He doesn't think his mom had any idea about the affair."

We're both quiet. Silence on my end of the phone, the buzz of the hospital on Luke's end.

"I was born during my mom's freshman year of college." Straight A's and she ended up transferring back to a local college. Because of me. "She died in a car accident sometime during her sophomore year of college." I take a breath. "But until she died, she was receiving monthly payments from Senator Gallagher."

"Wow," Luke says, his voice gentle. I know that voice. It's the *I feel sorry for you* voice. I've heard it my whole life. I hear a door close and it's suddenly quieter on Luke's end of the phone.

"Boyd works for the government. Apparently I came up during a background check. He'd never heard a word about me until then."

"Sophie, I…" He trails off.

He what? Feels sorry for me? Is appalled? Needs to cancel all future plans with me?

"I have to go, Sophie. I'll call you as soon as I can." The line goes dead.

I can't process anything right now. I'm… no one. I have a half-brother.

I already called my grandparents in Florida. They had no idea I had a sibling. I look at the silent phone in my hand and scroll through the contacts and make a call.

A short time later I'm walking into Shay's, a bar I've never been to before, located off campus. It's early when I walk in, quiet. Boyd is sitting in a booth and waves me over as soon as he sees me.

"Sophie," he says with a warm smile. He looks relieved to see me, like he was afraid I wasn't going to show up.

"Hey," I reply and take a seat. We stare at each other, neither of us knowing what to say, so I say the only thing possible. "I need a drink."

Boyd grins and signals to the waitress. "Thanks for calling, Sophie. I wasn't sure you would."

"I wasn't sure I would either."

He shrugs and gives me a sad smile. "Yeah." We're quiet then.

The waitress returns with our drinks and Boyd immediately orders shots for both of us. "You look like you need one," he says.

"Yeah," I whisper. "Tell me about him." Senator Gallagher died in his third term of office. I would have been about sixteen.

Boyd fills me in on things about our father I wouldn't be able to learn from the internet. He loved pineapple and hated chocolate. He made it a habit never to swear. He taught Boyd how to fish. I filled him in on my childhood with my grandparents. From what Boyd tells me he grew up very differently than I did. His upbringing sounds like what I imagined Luke's to be. Very privileged and formal.

The drinks keep arriving and I keep downing them, numbing my emotions. "I think I'm in love with Luke," I slur a short while later. "See?" I pull out my phone and find a picture of Luke and I, a selfie I took of us lying on his couch the weekend after Thanksgiving when we were watching *Elf*. I hold it up for Boyd to look at.

"That's great, Sophie. I'm happy for you," Boyd says quietly.

"He's a doctor." I hiccup. "And I'm classy." I laugh at my own joke. I'm funny. "Oh, shit, he's been calling," I say, looking at my phone. "We've been here a while."

"I'm sure he doesn't expect you to answer the second he calls," Boyd says reassuringly. "But maybe it's time to get a cab?"

"Probably," I agree, and then I rest my head on the table.

Twenty-Four

I awake to a pounding headache and too much light. I close my eyes again. I'm going to throw up. *Focus. Reach over and grab your trash can. Do not throw up on your bed, Sophie.*

I open my eyes slowly.

I have no idea where I am. Holy shit, I have never been this irresponsible in my life. The last twenty-four hours flash in front of me. The coffee shop, Boyd, Luke, Shay's Bar. I don't remember anything past Shay's. I need to call Luke back. Tears prick my eyes as I recall how good he's been to me, and I repaid him by ignoring his calls while I sat in a bar getting drunk with Boyd. I'm horrible.

"Hey, you're up." It's Boyd. I'm at Boyd's.

"Bathroom!" I blurt out, and Boyd points to a bathroom en-suite.

I stumble out of the bed and and make it to the bathroom just in time to throw up in the toilet. I sink to the bathroom floor and wipe my mouth. I feel like crap, I have vomit in my hair and I blew off Luke. I'm in a stranger's apartment. My brother's, sure, but he's still a stranger.

I stand up and examine myself in the mirror. I look awful. Being irresponsible does not look good on me. I close the toilet lid and sit before realizing my cell phone is in my pocket. Yes! 6:44 AM Friday morning. Eleven missed calls from Luke, Jean and Everly. Six voicemails. Thirty-four text messages.

I press the button to return Luke's call.

He answers on the first half ring. "Are you okay?"

"Yeah," I respond. "I'm—"

He cuts me off. "Where are you?"

He's so mad. I don't think my answer is going to help things. "I'm at Boyd's."

The silence is deafening.

"Where is Boyd's?"

"I'm sorry, Luke, I didn't mean to ignore your calls."

"Where. Is. Boyd's?"

"I don't know. I don't know where I am."

Silence.

"You're okay?" he asks again.

"Yes." I sigh. "I threw up but I'm fine. I'm in the bathroom."

"Jesus, Sophie, are you really this young?"

No, I want to say. *No.* I'm so mortified. It was stupid to get drunk with someone I don't know. I put my safety in the hands of a stranger. A drunk stranger. I'm lucky the only thing that happened to me was passing out and waking up with a hangover. What if Boyd had passed out too? I could have ended up anywhere. Stupid.

So I say nothing.

"Open the map app on your phone and tell me what street you're on."

I pull the phone away from my ear and do as I'm instructed. "I'm on South Street, somewhere between 13th and 15th."

"I'll be there in five minutes. Get the exact address from Boyd and text me."

The line goes dead. He hung up on me. I stand and look at my shitty reflection in the mirror again and use my hand to cup water from the faucet to rinse my mouth out.

I exit the bedroom and realize I'm in a large loft. A loft I have no recollection of seeing last night.

"My boyfriend is coming to pick me up."

"Luke," Boyd states.

"Uh, yeah. Was I talking about him last night?"

"Just a little." He laughs.

"I'm sorry you had to take care of me."

Boyd scoffs. "It was no problem."

"I need to text Luke your address." I wave my phone. "I can't believe I don't know where I'm at. So stupid."

"You're in college. You're entitled to a little fun."

I think our idea of fun is different, but I keep that to myself as I text Luke the address. "Have you lived here a long time?" I ask, looking around. There's not much in the way of personal items. It's a beautiful loft. Big, with views of the city.

He shrugs. "Less than a year." He tells me about the area while I wait for Luke. I realize we're less than a mile from Luke's place in Rittenhouse Square.

There's a knock on the door and I grab my coat and purse as Boyd opens the door.

I chance a glance at Luke. He looks exhausted. Boyd is speaking to him but Luke ignores him, his focus entirely on me.

"Wait in the car."

I say a quick goodbye to Boyd and get out of there as

fast as I can. The mood between Luke and I is so off and I do not want to argue with him in front of Boyd.

I reach Luke's car and place my hands on the passenger side roof, breathing in and out. I've made it through three and a half years of college without ever being this hungover. I will quite simply die if I vomit in Luke's luxury car.

I close my eyes and concentrate on breathing, waiting for the nausea to settle while wondering how my mother has managed to mess up my life nineteen years after leaving it. No, this isn't on her. It's on me. I'm the same person I was yesterday. Learning the name of the missing person on my birth certificate doesn't give me the right to throw away the life I've made for myself.

A hand comes to rest on my back. "You okay?"

I nod and Luke opens the passenger door and gets me settled before circling the car and getting behind the wheel. We drive in silence down Broad Street. It's just past 7:00 AM and traffic is picking up. The speeding up and slowing down are making me feel worse and I'm focused on not vomiting, so I don't immediately notice that Luke is taking me back to his Rittenhouse Square condo and not my dorm.

"I have class today," I protest as he pulls into the parking garage.

"Hopefully someone takes notes for you," Luke replies and pulls into his assigned parking space.

I open my mouth to argue, but I have to throw up again. I open the car door and make it to the trash can next to the elevator without a second to spare. Luke is there a moment later, hand on my back. The elevator opens and I assume he's pushed the button to call for it, but I realize it's someone exiting the elevator as Luke says, "Good morning, Mrs. Hudson." She replies and heels click away from us before I look up.

I am beyond humiliated. "I'm sorry," I say as Luke leads me into the empty elevator and pushes the button for the penthouse.

"For?"

"Everything. Specifically for looking like a drunk whore in front of your fancy neighbors."

"You don't look like a whore. Not one I'd bring home anyway."

I look at him and I know I have tears in my eyes about to fall but I'm trying to fight them.

"Hey, hey." He crosses the space between us in the elevator and wipes them away with his thumbs. "I'm kidding."

"Don't." I pull away and back up. "I smell disgusting."

He pulls me into him anyway and kisses the top of my head. "You do," he agrees. "But I don't care."

We take a shower together, but Luke does all the work, insisting on washing my hair and scrubbing me from head to toe. When we're done he hands me a toothbrush already loaded with a swipe of toothpaste and then returns with a glass of orange juice and two Advil before he tucks me under his covers, buck naked.

I think he's going to join me in bed but when I look up he's buttoning a crisp gray shirt. "You're going to work?" I try to keep the whine out of my voice.

"Yes, those of us not hungover have jobs to do." He loops a blue tie around his neck and begins twisting it into a perfect knot.

"Fine, leave me here and go to work. I'm sure you

have an appointment calendar full of women waiting for you to knock them up." I guess I'm done trying to keep the whining to myself.

Luke just smirks. "Thank you for reminding me," he says as he opens the drawer beside the bed and riffles around. "I need to pick up condoms today."

"Why?" I'm instantly on alert. We haven't used condoms since Thanksgiving. Does he not trust me anymore after I blacked out last night?

"How many times have you thrown up today"—he pauses—"so far?"

"Three."

"Did you take your pill this morning?"

"Yes." I see where he's going with this. "That I've already thrown back up." I fluff the pillow and turn on my side, watching him. "You're perfect for me."

"Why is that?" He shrugs into his suit coat. "Is it the way my cock is just a little too big to fit into your tight pussy and I have to stretch you out every time we fuck?"

Even though I'm hungover, the blood rushes to my pussy and I squirm under the sheets and press my thighs tighter together.

"Sophie?"

"Huh, what?" I'm so focused on not sticking my hand under the covers to rub myself while he's still in the room I've missed what he was saying.

"Why am I perfect for you?" He leans over the bed and kisses my forehead before rising and sliding a watch over his wrist. He smiles at me as his gaze drops to the place where my legs meet under the covers. He knows exactly what distracted me.

"You're the only one more paranoid than I am about

an unplanned pregnancy."

He pauses then for the briefest second and gnaws at his bottom lip. "Mrs. Geiger is coming today, so put some clothes on if you get out of bed. I've already informed her to skip the bedroom if you're still sleeping."

"I don't have any clothes here."

"You don't need clothes to sleep off your hangover and masturbate."

"Luke!" I hide my face behind my hands, which is apparently funny because he laughs.

"I've seen every last inch of you, Sophie. I've had your legs spread in stirrups with my hand in your pussy and you're embarrassed that I know damn well you're dying for me to leave so you can slide your hand under the covers and rub your clit until you come?"

"Yes," I mumble, face still behind my hands.

"Okay," Luke replies. "Do you want me to bring home a few supplies from the hospital so we can play kinky doctor tonight?"

Damn him. "Uh-huh," I mutter, still not looking at him.

"Use your words, Sophie, I need to hear you say it."

"Yes!" I sit up with the sheet clutched to my chest. "Yes, I want that." I throw a pillow at him. "Now go away."

Luke is laughing at me again as he turns to exit the bedroom.

"Wait."

He stops and turns back, halfway to the door. He raises an eyebrow in question.

"You're not mad?"

His jaw clenches. "I'm furious."

"Oh."

"But we're okay, Sophie. As long as you're safe and I know where you are, we're okay."

I nod.

"I'd like to turn you over my knee and spank the shit out of you, and before you get excited, I don't mean that erotically."

"I'm sorry," I whisper.

"I know," he replies.

* * *

Mrs. Geiger has washed and dried my clothing and I'm sitting in Luke's den when I hear him enter the condo that evening. He's hanging his coat in the front closet when I reach him. There's a black medical bag at his feet. I stop short and stare at it, my pussy clenching involuntarily. Clearing my throat, I ask Luke how his day was.

"Great," he responds. "Are you feeling better?"

"Much," I agree. My eyes dart to the bag.

Luke ignores the bag and steps around it to embrace me. "Should we go out to dinner?"

Dammit, no. "We could order pizza?" I suggest.

"No, we should go out."

Er. "How about Serafina?" We won't even need coats and we could be back in an hour if there's no wait.

"Hmm." Luke strokes my back, winding his fingers in my hair. "I was thinking Lombardi's. It's your favorite."

"That's forty-five minutes away!" I blurt out.

Luke steps back and frowns. "You've been cooped up inside all day, I thought you'd enjoy a drive and dinner out."

I am a horrible slut. All I can think about is what's in that bag and what Luke might do to me with it. I steal one last look at the bag and place a smile on my face. "You're right, that sounds nice."

Luke pauses, silently staring at me before one side of his mouth gives him away. "You don't want to go anywhere, you shameless hussy. You're practically gagging for me to pick up my little black bag and drag you by the hair into the bedroom."

I swallow. That's all true.

"Go to my office," he says instead.

Turns out his desk is a nice height for an impromptu exam table.

Twenty-Five

"I feel like I'm inside a snow globe!" I've got a blanket wrapped around me with my nose an inch from the terrace doors in Luke's bedroom. It's early, the sun still rising. Behind me Luke is still lying in bed, propped up on pillows, watching me.

Below me Philadelphia is covered in a blanket of snow with more falling. "It's beautiful." I turn and flash Luke a grin. "I love this view during the snow."

"I love you."

Did I hear that correctly? I take a moment and then turn my attention away from the snow swirling outside to focus on Luke. The comforter is resting at his waist, his chest bare.

"Come back to bed." He holds out a hand, beckoning me to him. I walk slowly back to bed but stop short of climbing back in. Did it just slip out? Did he mean to say it? Did he actually say it or did I mistake him? Crap. Now I'm just standing here and it's awkward. Should I tell him I couldn't hear him? No. It's too late for that. Now I'm nervous. I fidget and peek at him under my lashes.

He smirks. "You want me to say it again?"

"Yeah."

"Get your ass back in bed."

I sigh and roll my eyes as he laughs.

"I love you, Sophie," he repeats and I grin. "Now get your ass back in bed so I can show you how much."

"I want waffles," I say when I've regained the ability to speak. "I love waffles." I turn my head and grin at Luke.

"What else do you love?"

"Syrup."

"And?"

"Whipped cream."

"You can suck whipped cream off my cock if you want."

"I love sucking your cock."

"You'd love my cock in your ass even more."

"Maybe later." I wink.

He rolls on top of me then and pins my hands above my head while biting my neck. "Tease."

I buck underneath him, trying to get some friction on my clit, but he holds himself out of reach. "You're the tease, Doctor."

"You want it right now?" He moves both of my hands into one of his and uses his free hand to tease me. He slides a finger into me, coating it with my fluids and the come he just left in me, then slides it back into my ass.

I grunt or moan or whimper, I'm not sure what's coming out of my mouth. He's done this before with his finger and I like it. It's so wrong, forbidden, dirty. The sensations are different yet similar.

"Tell me you want it, Sophie."

"No." I shake my head, but I grind myself against his hand, encouraging him. He slides his finger out and adds a second as he slides back in.

"Mmm." I suck in my bottom lip and breathe out. Then Luke places his thumb on my clit and starts working me into a frenzy as he spreads his fingers inside of my ass, stretching me.

"You like it, baby?"

"Yes."

"Tell me you want my cock in your ass."

"No. Make me come."

"Such a demanding little hussy."

"Please, Luke!" I'm near inconsolable with need right now. I just came ten minutes ago but I am on edge again, I need the release.

Luke slides down my body and replaces his thumb with his mouth and sucks my clit between his teeth and bites gently. I come so hard I think I black out for a second. He pulls me to him and strokes the back of my head, then carries me from the bed to the walk-in shower where he proceeds to lather me in suds from head to toe. But it doesn't feel sexual. It just feels like being cared for.

I lean back, relaxing into Luke's chest with the water streaming over us. He washes my hair and then pulls my right arm up and bends it, placing my hand on the back of his neck. I massage his neck with my fingers as he lathers my breast with more suds. I sigh in contentment. I could stay in this shower all day if I didn't want waffles so badly.

Wait a minute. "Are you giving me a breast exam right now?" I ask.

Luke removes my right hand from his neck and replaces it with my left. "Yes."

I drop my arm. "Luke, that is so weird."

He picks my hand up and puts it back on his neck.

"Are you checking yourself every month?" He kisses my earlobe.

"No," I admit. *I'm twenty-one,* I want to add sulkily. *My boobs are perfect.*

"I don't want anything to happen to your perfect tits," he says as he continues. "They're mine."

Well, that was a pretty caveman thing to say. Yet I want to bend over and tell him to fuck me however he wants, so I guess it was effective. I turn around instead, interrupting his exam, and wrap my arms around his neck so I can pull him close enough to kiss. Then I push him away and step out of the shower.

"Hey," he protests.

"Waffles!" I call out as I dry off.

* * *

"We need to go shopping this weekend," Luke announces as he enters the kitchen a few minutes later.

"How domestic," I reply. "And here I thought Mrs. Geiger did all your shopping. You don't like to put lube on her grocery lists?"

He smacks my behind and then cages me in by placing both hands on the counter around me. "I have plenty of lube, you impertinent slut, just say the word." He kisses my neck then pushes off the counter. "You need a dress."

"For?" I ask.

"For the hospital gala. I told you about it."

"I'm certain you didn't." He didn't. Gina did.

"I'll need you to attend with me, Sophie. It's next weekend, so we need to find you a dress today."

"I'm meeting Boyd for lunch."

Luke's jaw ticks and he rubs his temple. "Why?"

"Why?" I question as I move a waffle from the maker to a plate. "He's my brother. Do I need a reason to have lunch with him?"

"Yes."

"Excuse me?" I stop with a measuring cup mid-pour over the waffle iron. Luke has moved to the Keurig and is watching the coffee drip into a mug.

"Was I unclear?"

I stare at him for a moment, dumbfounded, then finish pouring batter into the waffle maker before returning my attention to Luke. He's leaning against the counter, arms crossed, sipping from his mug.

"You're the boss of when I see my brother?"

"You're my responsibility."

I'm not sure if I should laugh or slap him. "Okay," I reply, drawing out the word. It's not okay, but Luke should be well versed at his age in the subtleties of the female response. There are about twenty definitions to the word okay when speaking to a woman.

"The last time you saw Boyd he got you drunk." Luke takes the plate I offer him and sits at the breakfast table in front of the window, but his eyes are on me. I remove the last waffle from the maker and drop it on my plate before sitting across from him.

"Boyd didn't get me drunk, I got myself drunk." I shake the can of whipped cream as I speak.

"He shouldn't have let you."

"Let me?" This conversation is getting more ridiculous by the second. "He doesn't own me, so why is he responsible for me?"

"Don't be cute, Sophie. He should have taken better care of you."

"Give him a break, Luke."

The fingers of Luke's left hand tap on the table. "I should get to know him then. What time is lunch?"

"I just walked right into that, didn't I?"

Luke smiles, smug in the knowledge that he got what he wanted. "You don't want to have lunch with both of us?"

I shrug. "Seems awkward."

He leans back in his chair and smirks. "I'm awkward?"

"You're never awkward and you know it." He's dressed for the day in a gray sweater and dark jeans. His hair is still damp from the shower and I want to sit on his lap and breathe in his aftershave while running my fingers through his hair, but we have things to do.

"Just be…" I trail off.

Luke raises a brow at me in question.

I sigh. "Nice."

"Whatever you want, Sophie." He's so agreeable. When he gets what he wants.

* * *

We walk to Joan Shepp, an upscale store just up the street from Luke's, to look for a dress for this gala. Well, Luke discusses options with a saleswoman—I just stand there fidgeting.

"She'll try all of these," Luke says, indicating the selection the saleswoman has pulled.

"Luke, no." I pull at his arm. I don't think I want any of these dresses. This store is making me nervous. I cannot afford to shop here.

"You haven't even tried them on yet. If you don't like any of these we can try another store after lunch."

Alone in a dressing room I undress and finger the price tags. I know a dress from Target isn't going to cut it in Luke's world, but I didn't realize the discrepancy was so great. Three thousand, six hundred and ninety-five dollars. Eighteen hundred dollars. Two thousand, four hundred and twenty-five dollars. Wait, here's a bargain— nine hundred and fifteen dollars. I'm sure Luke intends to pay, but I have no frame of reference for this. The nicest dress I've ever worn was to my prom and my prom date most certainly did not take me to the store and buy my dress.

There's a knock on the door. It's the saleswoman asking how the dresses are fitting and letting me know that the gentleman would like to see the fit.

I groan and pull the "cheap" dress off the hanger and slide it on. It's pretty, gray and slinky with a plunging neckline. I'm not wearing heels so it drags on the floor. I pinch the fabric at mid-thigh with my fingertips to raise the hem and walk out to find Luke. He's texting but stops and frowns when he sees my face.

"What's wrong? You don't like this one?" His gaze runs up and down my form. "It fits you perfectly."

I shake my head no. "Can we leave?" I ask quietly. Luke examines my face, waiting for more from me, but it's not coming.

"Okay," he agrees, but I can tell he's confused.

I strip out of the dress and change back into my jeans and sweater as quickly as possible and sigh in relief.

We exit the shop and walk towards Market Street.

We're meeting Boyd at the Capital Grille.

"Care to explain, Sophie?" Luke interrupts my thoughts as we walk. His eyes are focused ahead.

I shrug.

"Words, please."

"I don't want you to buy me a dress."

"Why not?"

I shrug again.

"Sophie." His tone indicates he's not amused.

"I just don't."

He's quiet then as we walk, our feet crunching over the shoveled sidewalks, cars swooshing past us on the street.

"Did you want me to find another date so you can stay home?"

"Like Gina?" I retort.

"What the hell does Gina have to do with this?" He sounds close to exhausted with me but I shrug again. I'm pretty sure based on the tick in his jaw that he'd be spanking my ass right now if we weren't in the middle of the street. I know I'm behaving like a brat, but I don't have any answers for Luke. I don't know how to express why the dress bothers me, but it does. Maybe it signifies how different we are. Buying expensive dresses and attending galas is not anything I see in my future, even after graduation.

"This is a black-tie event, Sophie, you need an appropriate dress if you're going to attend, and I'd like you to attend."

"I want to go with you." I trail off and then Luke gets a call, so I'm saved from elaborating. We've reached the Capital Grille on Chestnut, where we're meeting Boyd for lunch. Luke indicates I should go in while he finishes his call and I gladly take the opportunity to postpone this conversation.

Lunch is slightly nerve-racking. Luke spends the hour interrogating Boyd, which Boyd seems oblivious to, thankfully.

I'm trying to get to know Boyd. I'm not sure that we have much in common, but he's family. I don't know why Luke joined us, as he seems more interested in finding a reason why I shouldn't associate with Boyd than in getting to know him.

We part ways outside and I give Boyd a hug. I watch him walk away for a moment then turn and start walking with Luke in the opposite direction.

"I thought you agreed to be nice to Boyd, Luke."

"I wasn't nice?"

I roll my eyes and Luke raises his eyebrows.

"You were a little aggressive."

"Okay. I'll work on that." He takes my hand and we walk on in silence.

"What if I can't find a job right away?" I blurt out. "After graduation."

"I'll help you."

"Luke, no! That's not what I meant. And you're a doctor, how are you going to help me find an accounting job?"

"I meant financially, but I'm sure I could line up some interviews for you as well. Hospitals have plenty of accounting work."

"I meant, what if I have to waitress until I find a job? Are you still going to want to take me to charity galas? I'm a barista now, it's not any different than waitressing, I just make less money."

Luke pulls me over against a building, out of the path of people walking past, and puts his hand under my chin, tilting my face up to his. "Sophie, what are you getting at?"

"Why do you love me? I'm a college student and you're… you! You're a doctor with a trust fund and a fancy penthouse. You're cultured and associate with people who host charity events or sit on boards of companies. You have a housekeeper, Luke. I do my laundry in a coin-operated machine that I share with a hundred other students."

He tilts his head a little as he listens to me, then backs me into the brick wall of the store we're standing in front of and drops his forehead to mine and shuts me up with a kiss.

Twenty-Six

We finish our walk back to Luke's and he doesn't mention stopping anywhere to look at dresses. I'm not sure what to make of that, nor am I sure how to resolve my feelings about him paying for a dress, so I don't say anything. Entering the penthouse, I quickly realize we're not alone.

"Uncle Luke!" Bella comes tearing down the hallway and jumps onto Luke without slowing down. He laughs and tosses her in the air, which makes her squeal in delight. Seeing me she beams. "Soapy!" She wiggles her way back to the floor and grabs my hand. "We bring you Mommy's dresses!"

I let Bella lead me to Luke's bedroom, where I find Meredith hanging dresses in the empty walk-in closet closest to the door.

"Great, you're back from lunch." Meredith gives me a hug and Luke kisses her on the cheek. "Luke said you wanted to borrow a dress for the gala next weekend, so I brought over a bunch. I'll leave them all here as they won't fit me anytime soon," she says, patting her tiny baby bump. "If you don't like any of these I have tons more."

Luke is leaning against the door jamb. "You don't

191

mind?" I ask Meredith.

She scoffs. "Of course not. I have more dresses than I will ever be able to wear. I wouldn't even notice if you didn't return these, trust me."

"Thank you, Meredith," I say as I take in the rack of dresses. She must have had the concierge help her up, because there are eight dresses hanging neatly in a row. At least two of them will work. "These are perfect. I really appreciate it."

"Luke would have been happy to buy you a dress, you know. He'd buy you anything you wanted."

"I know," I respond, meeting her curious gaze. "I'm just not ready for that."

Meredith smiles. "Let me know which dress you decide on and I'll send over the shoes, bag and wrap to match."

We exit the unused closet and find Bella jumping on the bed with Luke keeping a close eye on her.

"Five little monkeys jumped on a bed," Bella chants. "One fell off and bumped her head! Luke said no more jumping on the bed!" Bella giggles hysterically. "Seven little monkeys jumped on a bed!" She continues on in non-numerical order.

"Come on, monkey, it's time to go home."

"Catch me, Uncle Luke," Bella yells as she launches herself off the bed with no warning. Luke catches her, of course, and swings her around before placing her on her feet, where she takes off running for the front door. I wonder if my life would be different if I'd been as confident as Bella at her age, surrounded by people who would never let me fall.

The front door shuts behind Meredith and Bella, and

Luke turns to me. "Is borrowing a dress agreeable?" He cocks one eyebrow.

"I love you back," I reply instead.

His eyes spark before his lips twitch in a grin. "The trick was borrowing things for you?"

"I'm curious about anal."

His eyes positively light up. "I can help you with that," he responds, picking me up by the waist so that I wrap my legs around him as he walks us back to the bedroom. "We can call it a loan from your pussy to your ass, if this borrowing thing is what gets you hot."

I laugh at that before he wraps a hand into my hair and tugs hard, pulling at my scalp. The slight pain sends a trail of want straight down my core, ending in a throb between my legs. I return the favor, placing both of my hands in his thick hair and tugging hard. He groans into my mouth. I love it when he groans. I love all the noises he makes when we're together. He's normally so polished, controlled. Knowing I make him lose himself, it's intoxicating.

His fascination with sticking it in my ass thrills me, if I'm being honest. It's like he can't get enough of me, like he wants to be inside of me in every way possible. It's so taboo, yet he doesn't flinch at sticking his finger in my back end, or his tongue. I want to experience his cock there too.

"Luke, I want you to come in my ass, okay?" I tug his head back and look in his eyes. "I want to feel you dripping out of me when we're done."

"You filthy little bitch, you're gonna be the death of me."

He stands me next to the bed and pulls my sweater off

over my head while I scramble to remove his. He undoes my pants next, pushing me back on the bed once they've cleared my hips and then dragging them the remaining way down my legs with my panties.

I move to scoot back on the bed but he stops me with one word. "Stay." My ass is on the edge of the bed, my feet on the floor as he leans forward and unsnaps my bra.

"Hands," he says and I'm confused by the request but I hold them up. He pushes my palms together then uses my bra to bind my hands before pushing me onto my back and raising my legs off the floor. He's got me flat on my back, arms restrained over my head as he bends me in half, my spread knees on either side of my head.

"Jesus, look at you." His eyes travel over my body. I'm not hard to see in this position. It's late afternoon and every window shade is open. The penthouse height provides privacy that the sunlight does not. I squirm under his gaze. I don't care how many times Luke's fucked me or how much pussy he's seen in his life, being spread out this baldly makes my heart race in some combination of voyeuristic enjoyment and insecurity.

He drops his pants and palms his thick length, running his hand up and down. He's not gentle with himself, his grip firm, exactly like he instructs me to grip him in my small hands when I get the chance. "Use both hands, Sophie," he'd say. "Be firm, your cunt is tighter than your grip."

Luke hasn't touched me yet, just keeps his eyes between my legs, my body open to his view as he touches himself. I feel wetness gather at my entrance, about to spill over, and I know Luke sees it too because he groans and drops to his knees besides the bed and rims my entrance with his tongue, wiping me clean.

I arch my back off the bed. His face between my thighs is my undoing. He grips my already spread cheeks and spreads them wider, further opening my asshole to him.

"You like my tongue in your ass, don't you?" he murmurs as he rims my asshole with his tongue.

I feel a slap against my open pussy when I don't respond and I jump, the added blood flow making me insane. "Yes, I love it, Luke. You know I love it."

"Of course I know, but I enjoy hearing you admit it."

"I love how you touch me, Luke. I always feel safe even when you're doing things to me that should scare me."

He kisses the insides of my thighs as I talk. "Thank you," he says, a second before running his tongue flat across my asshole and sliding two thick fingers in my pussy. "I think you like my fingers in you almost as much as you like my cock. Don't you?"

"I prefer your dick, but your fingers are magic," I answer before he can dream up another way to tease me for not responding.

"I'm going to fuck you so hard your entire body will hurt tomorrow."

"Yes," I agree and buck my hips against his hand, trying to get pressure on my clit.

"I love your tight holes, baby. I love that I'm the only one who's been in them." He pumps his fingers in and out. "You're awfully pure for such a little slut."

I come then, his fingers working that magic spot inside of me to perfection, his dirty words sending me over the edge. He removes his fingers and plunges them into my behind, coated in my own come. The sudden intrusion is painful, my body shocked between pleasure from my orgasm and pain from my rectum. It intensifies my orgasm to a point I'm not sure I can handle and I cry out.

"Shh, babe, you're fine," Luke consoles me, kissing my breasts as he continues stretching my ass with his fingers. He's scissoring his fingers in my ass wider than he's done before. It burns, but the pain feels good. He bites my nipple hard as he widens the stretch and my body isn't sure which pain to focus on.

Withdrawing his fingers from my ass, Luke yanks me to a sitting position and frees my hands from their constraints. "Face down, ass up." He slaps my ass hard as I turn over with my knees to the edge of the bed, ass in the air and propped on my elbows. It's a position I'm familiar with.

Luke pulls a tube of lube from the nightstand. I know this lube well. It's been taunting me from the nightstand since the first time I snooped through Luke's drawers back in October. The condom supply ran low once we started going bare. He replenished those after my hangover-induced vomiting last month, but the lube remained constant. Luke's mentioned anal on and off and I'm not naive enough to discount the fact that the lube was here before me.

Luke can stick his fingers in my ass and make all the comments he wants about fucking it, but I don't feel pressured. I'm curious. Everything Luke does to me feels good. Even when it's a little painful, it's good. I enjoy his fingers in my ass when his mouth is on my clit, that's for sure. And I know he enjoys the occasional finger in his ass while his cock is down my throat.

He lines up behind me with the unopened lube still in his hand and slides into me in one thrust as he flips the top on the lube and coats two fingers.

"I'm gonna finger-fuck your ass while I fuck your pussy," he tells me as he slips a finger into my ass. "You feel that? I can feel my cock with my finger from inside your tight ass." He thrusts his penis deep and stills, sliding his finger back and forth in my anal passage where it aligns with his dick. It's so damn tight like this, with both holes occupied. He pours more lube directly into my back end and slides a second finger in. I flinch and lurch forward on the bed.

"Stay." Luke slaps the side of my thigh with his free hand.

"Wait." I twist and turn my head to look at him. "Wait, I have a question."

He stills for a moment then withdraws his fingers, followed by his cock, then reaches into the nightstand for a tissue and wipes his fingers, but keeps his eyes on mine. "What is it, Sophie?"

"Um." I bite my lip then blow out a breath. "Will it go back?"

Luke remains almost expressionless but cocks an eyebrow. How does he not know what I mean? "Will my asshole go back to normal?" I nod towards his dick. "You're really large. Will I, um, still poop normal after this?"

The room is dead silent then. A few seconds tick by like minutes and then Luke loses it laughing. He sits on the edge of the bed with his elbows on this knees, shaking. "Christ, Sophie."

"You asshole! You're laughing at me? You're the genius doctor. 'Ask me anything, Sophie. Don't be shy, Sophie.'" I'm still on my knees, looking at him over my shoulder. I flip and sit on my butt, drawing my knees to my chest. "Liar!" I shoot at him.

"Sophie." His tone is warning.

"Would you prefer if I got answers from my girlfriends? 'Hey, girls, Luke is hung like a donkey and he wants to put it in my ass. What should I expect?'" I scoot to the edge of the bed. "I'll call Jean right now, you jerk." I start to get up but Luke grabs me and pulls me onto his lap.

"I'm sorry, baby," he says and taps me on the nose with his finger. "You're right, I just thought your questions would be verbalized before I was about to stick my dick in your ass."

I place my palm on his chest and look up into his face. Waiting.

He clears his throat. "Your asshole will be fine. With proper stretching and lubrication your anal tract will not be damaged and you will continue to…"—he pauses, searching for my terminology—"poop just fine. But stretching and lube are essential. Got it?"

I nod.

"Good. Now I need a minute. I don't think I can fuck you anywhere just yet."

My eyes widen and I slap his chest with my open palm before sliding to the floor between his knees and grasping his cock. It's still hard, but not fully. I pump it with a firm hand. "We are having anal. Jerk."

Luke smirks. "Did you just order me to violate your ass?"

"I did and you will."

Twenty-Seven

"Suck me," he directs.

I open my mouth over the tip of him and he grabs the back of my head and shoves himself in farther. Winding his hand into my hair, he fucks my mouth, sliding my head over his shaft and directing me when he wants additional suction or tongue before yanking me off with a pop.

"There's an ACE bandage in my medicine cabinet. Go get it."

I return from the bathroom with the bandage roll and he holds out his hand. I drop the roll in his hand and wonder where he's going with this. I bite my bottom lip to hide my grin.

"You're way too confident for someone about to get their ass reamed."

The grin threatening to pull at my cheeks dissipates.

He unwinds one end of the bandage and wraps it around the opposite hand before pulling it taut. "I should gag you. I should fuck your ass with you bound and gagged with no way to say no."

I swallow, but I don't respond or move.

"But that would be a punishment for me, not you, because I like to hear you. I like to hear that little whimper you make when I stretch your pussy open and again when I bottom out against your cervix." He trails a fingertip along the shell of my ear and I do my best to stay still and listen without dissolving into a puddle of need on the spot. "Because after that whimper you always say, 'More, Luke. More, more, more.' I don't think you even know you're saying it."

He's right. I didn't.

"So I can't gag you."

"No," I agree. "That wouldn't be fun."

"On the bed, head on a pillow."

I scramble onto the bed, lie on my back and wait. Luke moves onto the bed and spreads my thighs so he's kneeling between them, then raises my right leg and wraps the bandage several times around my bent knee before attaching the bandage to the headboard. My leg is now raised at a ninety-degree angle. He repeats the configuration on my left knee and then props two pillows beneath my butt.

"Hold onto the headboard," he instructs and I reach over my head to grasp a wooden slat with both hands. "If you move your hands I'll stop before you come. Understand?"

I nod. I'm on my back with my knees up and spread, the position not much different from the time I was spread out on Luke's exam table. He grabs the lube and drips it directly onto my skin, then rims the opening with the tip of a finger. The lube is cool against my skin. His swirling finger on the sensitive tissue is making my pussy throb. He pushes a single finger into my ass and starts the process of stretching me again.

"You like my finger in your ass, don't you?"

"You're so dirty." He's making me crazy with his filthy mouth.

"You love it."

"I love you," I reply. I love the look in his eyes when I say it.

"I love you all trussed up like this. I can do whatever I want to you." He palms my breast with his other hand and then rolls the nipple between his finger and thumb then twists as he slides another finger inside of me. "You look obscene. Your sweet little backside is stretched around my fingers. Your pussy is so wet it's dripping. I'm almost sad I'm not fucking your cunt, but I can't wait any longer to see your ass stretched around my dick."

My hands twitch on the headboard. I want to touch him so badly. I want him to shove it in and lean over me so I can run my hands up and down his chest. I don't know where he finds the time to keep himself in the shape he does, but I can't get enough of his body.

He withdraws his fingers and, leaning forward, places a hand on the headboard above me to brace himself. "Hold out your hand," he says as he flips the cap on the lube.

I drop one of my hands from the headboard and hold it out, palm up. He pours a generous amount of lube into my waiting hand. "Lube my dick, Sophie."

I grasp him with my slick hand, running the lube up and down the length of him, then slide my palm across the tip.

"Better do a good job. I'm not stopping this time until my dick is buried in your ass."

My pussy clenches and I examine the penis in my hand. It's way bigger than two of his fingers. "More lube, please." I hold up my palm.

Luke smirks as he flips the lid again. I coat him liberally and place my hand back on the headboard as he places himself against me. I hold my breath and clench involuntarily.

"Relax, babe. Breathe." Luke places his thumb on my clit. "You're so beautiful. I love seeing you like this, spread out below me, filled with me." He's rubbing firmly with his thumb as he pops the head of his penis past my resistance point. I moan—I can't not as I briefly close my eyes against the burn. It hurts, but I want to watch him.

"Look at you," he breathes, eyes fixed on our joined bodies. "You look so perfect stretched around my cock, you filthy girl. Next weekend I'm going to dress you up in couture and parade you in front of my colleagues, but I'll be thinking about my cock buried in your ass the entire time. I'll be thinking about how graceful and lovely you are in public and what a dirty hussy you are in private." He slides in further. The burn feels good now that he's past the initial push. It feels so wrong, but right at the same time. The pressure is crazy intense and I feel so kinky. I clench again and Luke stops thumbing my clit to rim my pussy with his fingertip. "You dirty gorgeous girl, you're loving my cock in your ass so much your pussy is leaking."

"Luke, my clit. Please, please, please," I beg.

He laughs. "You do it. Go ahead, you can move your hands to touch yourself."

I'm only too happy with those instructions and I move my hand down and rub myself with the tips of my first two fingers. I'm shaking it feels so different.

He slides in farther and leans over me, propping his

weight on his arms. "You're so fucking hot and tight around my cock. It's killing me not to blow my load in you right now." He slides in and out. "How does it feel?"

"I like it, Luke. It's so wrong that it feels so good."

"It's never wrong when I'm inside you. Never." He kisses me then, briefly, before locking his elbows above me and increasing the pace slightly. "It's different between us, Sophie. You have no idea."

I don't want to know what any of this is like with anyone else, but I don't say it. This is so intense, having him inside of me like this. It's always intense between us—sex will always be personal for me—but this is something else altogether. He's inside of me in a way that's not quite natural, but so intimate. The sensations are different.

"It's good? You're okay?" Luke asks above me, his eyes searching mine. "Tell me how it feels for you."

"It's so tight, I feel everything." It's hard to talk, I'm so worked up. "It feels sensitive, but I'm okay," I offer. "I feel full, really full and it feels incredible when you slide back in."

He groans. "I'm going to come so hard in your ass. You're going to feel me all night." He slides his hand past mine and slips a finger inside me. "Should I take you out for dinner tonight? With my come dripping out of your bottom?"

"Luke, I'm close. I'm so close."

"I know." He moves his finger inside of me while continuing to thrust in my ass. I come then, my body tightening around his cock so hard it hurts. "Fuck, Sophie." He stills above me for a moment then jerks his hips as his orgasm erupts.

He drops his arms and pulls me to his chest. It's a little hard to breathe, but I'm barely coherent anyway. "I should untie you," he murmurs, still weighing me down with his body pressed to mine.

"Hmm." I flex my toes. "You don't want to keep me tied up in one of your weird empty bedrooms as a sex slave?"

"I can't keep you," he says just as his phone rings. "Christ." He closes his eyes for a moment with his forehead pressed to mine, then kisses me lightly on the lips, pulls out of my ass and grabs the phone with a short, "Dr. Miller."

I'm sweaty and sore and I can feel his come leaking out of my ass and onto the pillow he propped under me. I really hope Mrs. Geiger is well compensated.

Luke is sitting on the edge of the bed talking about a 3D ultrasound and weeks of gestation as I realize I can reach the end of the ACE bandage knotted to the headboard, so I set about untying myself. My feet are on the floor before Luke realizes I've moved.

"I have to call you back." Luke ends the call abruptly and grabs my wrist, pulling me back to him. He places his hands on my hips and kisses my stomach. "I'm sorry," he tells me.

"It's fine." I mean, it's not great, but it's fine. I expected a little more attention post-anal, but babies don't birth themselves, apparently. I shift, pressing my legs together.

Luke sits back and eyes me. "Are you okay? Did I hurt you? Lie down, let me look." He's all Dr. Miller right now.

"Eww, no! You're not giving me an exam right now."

I step out of his reach.

He doesn't look impressed with my refusal. "So we can play gynecologist when it suits you, but I can't look at you when you may actually need assistance?"

"You got that right. Plus, I'm *fine*." I stress the last word. "I'm fidgeting because your come is leaking out of my ass and down my leg. Are you happy now?" I move towards the bathroom.

He grins and follows me, wrapping an arm around me as I reach into the shower and turn it on.

"I need a washcloth," I say as he attempts to back me into the shower. He reaches between my legs and runs his hand across my wet skin.

"You sure do," he replies and continues to smear his come around my thighs.

"Doesn't somebody's fetus need your attention?" I remind him.

He murmurs an agreement. "I have to run over to the hospital. Come with me and we can have dinner at Lombardi's after."

"I do love their chicken piccata."

Twenty-Eight

"Why can't they fundraise in June?" I ask Luke. "It's freezing."

We're on our way to the Baldwin Memorial Hospital Charity Gala. He glances at me across the back seat and smiles.

"Too much competition. There are events all year for one charity or another. The summer months are filled with events and golf outings."

"Explain to me again how this makes sense financially. Thousands of dollars are spent on designer clothing and event space. Wouldn't the charity make more if everyone just sent a check?"

"There's a silent auction too," Luke reminds me.

"Couldn't we all agree to meet at a bowling alley in jeans and donate the money spent on clothing and event space to the charity instead?"

Luke laughs as the courtesy town car of his condo building turns right onto Chestnut, headed towards the Ritz Carlton down the street. It's a half mile from his condo but it's January and I'm in heels with a wrap jacket over my short dress. "You're refreshing, Sophie."

Am I? I was serious. This dress I'm borrowing cost a fortune and it's probably been worn twice, including tonight. It's not financially sensible.

The town car pulls under the awning covering the entrance to the hotel and my door is opened as soon as the car comes to a complete stop. Luke walks around the car and ushers me to the door so we're only outside for a few moments.

I don't want to be here. I did not grow up attending charity functions. I grew up raising money for charity by selling candy bars or participating in car washes.

"You're not going to leave me alone, right?" I say, pulling the matching shawl tighter. The dress is lovely, if not practical. It's white, ending a few inches above my knees. The dress has gorgeous crystal detailing down a vee-neck front and wrapped around the waist. The look is completed with strappy silver stilettos and drop earrings, again loans from Meredith.

Luke's brow is furrowed as he glances at me. "Don't be intimidated, Sophie. They're just people. And they don't get to see me naked." He whispers the last part in my ear.

"Not most of them, no," I agree.

"I had no idea you were so jealous, doll," he says, his eyes dancing. "If you want, I'll let you rake your nails down my back later."

I glance at my nails, considering it. Meredith and I spent the afternoon at a spa getting ready. Hair, makeup and nails. Getting ready for the event was fun and Meredith assured me I looked perfect.

Luke tried to initiate a quickie as I was getting dressed and I shot him down for, I think, the first time ever. No way was he messing me up before we left. He laughed at me when I shrieked, "No way," then smacked my ass and promised me, "Later."

The guy really is obsessed with slapping my behind.

Luke hands our coats over at the coat check while I stand holding the tiny clutch that matches the dress. As Luke is returning to my side he's stopped by a couple about his age, the woman obviously pregnant. I'm not that familiar with pregnant women, but I'd estimate her to be a little bit farther along than Meredith, who I know is four months.

The woman is positively glowing. At Luke. Her companion shakes Luke's hand before Luke introduces them as Dr. Davis and his wife, Sarah.

"When is your due date?" Luke asks them.

"June first," Sarah replies, beaming. "We can't thank you enough. I still can't believe I'm finally pregnant," she says, patting her little bump.

"I'm happy for you both," Luke says, placing a hand on my waist and pulling me closer to him.

He's her doctor, I realize. I know what Luke does for a living but I've never considered coming face to face with one of his patients. Is it weird? Or am I thinking like a sixteen-year-old girl?

Luke leads me into the cocktail portion of the evening. There are waiters walking the room offering champagne and appetizers. The perimeter of the room is lined with tables for the silent auction. The entire room screams wealth, from the chandeliers overhead to the expensive footwear adorning the attendees' feet.

Luke accepts a glass of champagne from a passing waiter and hands it to me.

"None for you?" I ask, taking a sip.

"I'm on call," he replies and guides me to one of the

JANA ASTON

tables. "Let's find something fun to bid on."

"We can bid on porn?" I ask sweetly and take another sip. I swear I see his hand twitch. He wants to swat my behind for that comment so bad, but he can't during a charity event in a room full of his peers.

When I think I can look at him without laughing I glance his way. He leans in and pulls me closer with a hand to the small of my back.

"I hope you don't have anything important happening at school on Monday, because I'm going to spend the remainder of this weekend fucking you until you can't walk comfortably." He steps back with a smug smile, content in the knowledge that he knows exactly what to do to my body to keep me in bed all weekend, willingly.

I spy Meredith and Alexander approaching, so I plaster the most innocent expression I can muster on my face and smile.

"I hope we're not interrupting," Meredith says, giving each of us a hug.

"Not at all," I reply. "I was just telling Luke how much I'm looking forward to Monday."

Luke coughs and Meredith looks confused. "Monday?"

"Yes, it's Martin Luther King Day, so classes are cancelled. I'm really looking forward to sleeping in and a long soak in the tub." I smile at Luke and his eyes narrow just enough for me to catch it.

"The dress looks even better on you than I'd imagined," Meredith says, eyeing me. "You'll have to keep it. I can't wear it again now that I've seen how much better it looks on you."

"Thank you for the loan, but I'm returning everything

to you next week. This is much too fancy to wear to class," I joke.

We part ways with Meredith and Alexander after a few minutes of chatting and walk the room, Luke dropping little slips of paper into the bid boxes for several auction items. He pauses in front of a display for a week at the Ritz Carlton Waikiki, staring at it with more thought than a trip to Hawaii really requires.

The doors open to the main event space a few minutes later and we make our way in and find our assigned table. I realize quickly that we are sitting with Luke's family. It's almost an exact repeat of Thanksgiving, minus Bella and the Holletts. His mom and dad are already seated, with his aunt and uncle to their right. Place cards indicate that I am sitting between Luke and his father, just like Thanksgiving.

We take our seats as Meredith and Alexander arrive to complete our table of eight. Meredith is seated on the other side of Luke so I can't even see her. Why did Luke bring me to this?

Waiters arrive and fill wine glasses moments before more waiters arrive with a soup course. I'm so nervous. This is worse than Thanksgiving. This time I know his parents are awful and I'm out of my element wearing couture in front of a place setting with way too much silverware. Plus, soup? I'm wearing a three-thousand-dollar white dress. I use the soup spoon to stir the contents of the bowl I have no intention of consuming, while around me the room is buzzing with chatter and the clinking of silverware.

For the tenth time this week I wonder how this event is benefiting anyone.

Someone stops by to say hello to Luke as Luke's father asks me to pass the salt. I move the salt and pepper over and place it in front of him, smiling out of politeness. The elder Dr. Miller is a handsome man. He radiates authority, but his eyes lack the warmth of Luke's. I can't imagine this man laughing at anything.

"You're graduating this spring?" This question is from Luke's father. I'm surprised that he's speaking to me.

"I am," I reply.

"Are you planning on working?" he questions.

"Of course," I reply, confused by the question.

"Good. You're a smart girl, Miss Tisdale. You're capable of being more than my son's trophy fuck."

I feel like he just punched me in the gut. A trophy fuck? His parents are even more awful than I thought.

"Sophie?" Luke is trying to get my attention. I turn in my seat back to him. "I wanted to introduce you to one of my colleagues, Dr. New."

I shake the hand offered to me and holy crap if this guy doesn't look like he could be Henry Cavill's older brother. This lookalike appears to be a few years older than Luke, maybe forty or forty-five. I'm not attracted to him, but he's a very attractive man. I imagine Luke will only get better-looking in the next decade as well, as many men tend to do as they age.

There seems to be a comradeliness between them, as if they've been friends for years, an idea that is confirmed when Dr. New brings up Luke's golf scores from this past summer.

"Justin's daughter Michelle was just accepted at Penn," Luke tells me, then explains to Dr. New that I am graduating from Penn this spring.

I see the flash of surprise on Dr. New's face for a brief moment before he hides it. I hope I hid my surprise as well as he did. Luke's friend has a daughter only a few years younger than me. That's... weird.

"So, ah..." Dr. New pauses. "You've enjoyed Penn?"

"I love it there. I'll be sad to graduate and leave the campus."

"Oh, do you live on campus?" His eyes move to Luke and back to me. His face may not betray what he's thinking, but I can tell he's curious about Luke and I.

"I do. I live in Jacobsen." I shrug. "It's convenient being on campus and cheaper than an off-campus apartment."

"Michelle wants an off-campus apartment. I told her we'll discuss it sophomore year." Dr. New smiles ruefully. "It's bad enough I've got to let her live in a co-ed dorm, I'm sure as shit not setting her up in an apartment off campus." He shakes his head. "Tell me she will be too busy studying and the boys never leave their own floors. Lie to me, please."

I glance at Luke, remembering our tryst in my dorm room weeks ago, before fixing a smile on my face. "Well, I never had any boys in my room freshman year, Dr. New. So there's hope."

"Thank you for humoring me," he says, not realizing I'm telling him the truth. "So what are your plans after graduation?" He seems genuinely interested. Luke looks interested in my response as well. It occurs to me then that we haven't discussed my plans. We don't discuss the future at all, come to think of it. He only invited me to this event last week.

"I'm hoping to find a job in corporate accounting," I

respond.

"Ah, an accounting major. Very practical."

"Exactly," I agree. "I love the practicality of accounting, both as a major and a career. I like the structure of it."

"Well, good luck on finding a position you're happy with. Lots of great companies in Philly." He pauses. "New York as well."

My eyes flick over to Luke's at the mention of New York, but his face gives nothing away. "Yes," I agree. "Lots of job opportunities."

Dr. New leaves us then as the waiters whisk away the soup course. Luke takes my hand under the table and runs his thumb over the back of my hand. The small moment of intimacy helps calm me. I take a breath and look up to see yet another couple stopping by to say hello to Luke.

Luke introduces them to me and then the woman pulls out a cell phone from her small bag and shoves it in front of Luke.

"Julie just turned three," she beams, then leans in to swipe the screen, changing the picture on the phone in Luke's hand. "She's so smart. She loves books and robots." She laughs. "We have no idea why, but the kid loves robots."

"You might have a future scientist or astronaut on your hands," Luke says, handing the phone back.

"Another satisfied customer," I say as the couple departs and the waiters arrive with the main course.

Luke glances at me before responding. "Does that bother you?"

I shrug. "You sure get a lot of business in house."

WRONG

"And?" Luke's voice has a warning to it that I don't appreciate. At all.

"And I was your patient once too."

"Sophie, enough." Luke shuts down the conversation with those two words.

I look at the meal in front of me and suddenly I'm not interested in eating. This room feels too hot and too loud and I just want out.

"Excuse me." I push back from the table and Luke stands to assist me. "I'm going to the restroom."

Luke's jaw ticks in annoyance. That's fine, I'm annoyed with him too. I make my way past waiters and fellow guests milling about and exit the ballroom space into a hotel corridor. I sigh in relief. I was starting to feel a little queasy in that room, but I feel fine now that I'm not surrounded by a crowd. There's a women's restroom across the hall and I make a beeline for it. I just want a place to hide out for a few minutes and collect myself.

There's a pregnant woman washing her hands when I enter. I duck past her into a stall before I'm tempted to ask her if her bump is courtesy of Luke as well. I know I am behaving like a little bitch right now. I'm disgusted with myself, yet I'm still feeling just bitchy enough to refuse to go out there and apologize.

I hear the woman finish up at the sink and exit the bathroom. I'm alone now, so I figure hiding in a stall is more pathetic than necessary. I leave the safety of the stall while digging around in my clutch for the lipstick I brought with. I'm in the middle of reapplying when the bathroom door swings open and Gina breezes in.

I have to admit I'm slightly surprised to see her here. Specifically in this bathroom. I'd have thought she'd

217

prefer to slip into my empty chair and keep Luke company while she has the chance.

"Sophie, darling!" She does a scan of the bathroom, confirming that we're alone. "You look breathtaking in that dress."

I'm confused. Is this woman bipolar? She looks stunning herself, her long red hair curled to perfection and trailing over one shoulder. She's in a platinum-colored gown, floor-length with a scoop neckline and a pear-shaped diamond pendant hanging from her throat.

"Gina." I nod in greeting.

She turns to the mirror and fingers the diamond pendant, centering it on her chest.

"That's a beautiful necklace," I compliment her. If she's being nice, I can be nice. Being catty isn't in my nature anyway. Maybe she's found someone new and I won't have to deal with her jealous behavior at these events. Assuming Luke brings me to more of them.

"Luke bought it for me," she replies and opens her own clutch.

I guess we're not done being catty. "Okay," I say and roll my eyes. This woman is something else.

She smirks at me in the mirror. "Luke bought me the nicest jewelry when we were together. I'm looking forward to seeing what he comes up with for my second engagement ring."

I look at her for a moment. "So you're crazy then?"

She arranges her face into a pout and examines her reflection in the mirror. "That's not kind, Sophie. I don't think Luke would want you calling his patients crazy."

"I'm not. I'm calling *you* crazy," I say. And as I do, as the word leaves my mouth, I realize she's his patient.

Why in the ever-loving hell would he agree to treat her? I'm almost blind with rage, that's how angry I am.

"Your plan is to win him back by having him treat you for infertility?" I'm dumbfounded. How does this make sense?

I can't think straight, I'm so pissed about Luke touching her. I know he's a doctor, I know this. Encountering women at events that he's treated is weird enough, but his ex-fiancée?

"Something like that," she replies with a smug smirk.

I want to strangle this bitch with my bare hands. What's involved with fertility treatment? He's probably inseminated her. I wonder who her donor is. I'm picturing her flat on her back with her feet in stirrups and Luke between her legs.

Can I kill her with a lipstick tube? What else do I have in my clutch?

"Why is he helping you?" I'm incredulous. I know they're colleagues, but she's his ex-fiancée. Why wouldn't he refer her to another doctor?

"You don't know anything, do you?"

What don't I know? "I know Luke is leaving here with me and I know you're crazy."

"Wrong and wrong," she laughs. "I'm very fragile, Sophie, from all the fertility drugs." She actually sniffs. "And Luke will be leaving with me. In the next ten minutes."

I'm so worked up I feel queasy again. "Get out," I tell her. "Get the hell out of my sight, you crazy bitch."

"Tsk, tsk. Language, Sophie." Gina breezes out the door. She's not gone a second too soon, because tears fall down my cheeks a second later.

What is going on? What is he doing with her? I feel stupid. Left out and stupid. I've spent my limited adult life dating a man who was attracted to men, a man who wanted to film me without my consent, and Luke. Clearly my character-judging skills are off.

I grab some tissue and clean myself up. I will not have a breakdown in this bathroom. Gina's probably lying, yet things are starting to fall into place. I remember her stopping by Luke's condo the weekend after Thanksgiving in tears and Luke telling her to call his office the following week.

Forget it, I tell myself. I am not thinking of this right now. I am going back out there with a smile on my face and I'll talk to Luke about all this later.

I exit the bathroom and cross the corridor to the ballroom space and swing open the door.

I'm so disheartened with Luke right now. I don't think I know him at all. I feel… misled somehow.

I enter the ballroom while taking a deep breath. Maybe he has some social disorder that prevents him from realizing that he's wrong about Gina.

Two steps into the room I almost trip over my stilettos. Luke's seat is empty, because he's walking away, with his hand on Gina's back.

I turn around and exit the door I just came through and start walking. I'm not sure where I'm going except in the opposite direction of Luke and Gina. I have to get out of here. We arrived through an event entrance, that's the direction that Luke and Gina are walking. I'm sure I can catch a cab at the main entrance so I won't have to bump into them. I check my clutch to reassure myself that my ID and credit card are still there. I can get home with that.

I keep walking until I find my way to the main lobby of the Ritz Carlton and head straight outside for a cab, only then realizing I don't have Meredith's shawl. Luckily there's a line of cabs out front waiting for fares and the bellhop has me in one in moments.

I feel like I should cry, but I'm numb.

"Where to, miss?" the cab driver wants to know as he pulls into traffic and my cell phone starts ringing.

"Spruce and 38th," I tell him, giving him the directions to my dorm while glancing at my phone, the screen indicating a call from Luke. I hit ignore and then turn the phone off and toss it back in my bag.

Twenty-Nine

I bawl my eyes out in the back of that cab, big ugly tears that have the driver staring at me though the rearview mirror until I lie down on the seat so he can't see me anymore. I'm tired. When did my life become so derailed? I'm graduating this spring with an honors degree from an Ivy League college. I am not a trophy fuck.

"Which building, miss?" the cabbie asks, turning onto Spruce.

I sit up and wipe my face with my hand. "Jacobsen, ahead on the left." I slide my credit card through the card scanner attached to the Plexiglas window separating the driver from the back seat.

I move as fast as I can on heels to the front door of Jacobsen in my short sleeveless dress, chilled instantly in just a few steps. Does this classify as a walk of shame if it's still evening? I feel conspicuous dressed like this surrounded by a sea of jeans, Uggs and down-filled jackets. My heels clicking across the lobby floor sound like gunshots to my ears. I can't wait to get to my room and replace them with comfort socks and crawl into bed.

I'm about to jab the elevator button when I catch something from the corner of my eye. Mike. He's on one of the sofas in the lobby charming a girl I know from the building. I see red. There are plenty of girls on this campus, plenty of dorms other than mine where Mike can troll for gullible girls. I can't help them all, but I can help this one.

I stomp over to the sofa intent on interrupting. "Saylor," I call out, getting the girl's attention. She's a sophomore. I've tutored her in freshman accounting.

She looks up, surprise crossing her face before being replaced with concern. I'm not sure if the concern is for me or her, since I'm a disheveled mess with mascara streaked down my face.

"Sophie, are you okay?" Saylor pushes away from Mike and scoots to the edge of the sofa closer to me.

"I'm fine," I reply, glaring at Mike. "Are you with him?"

"Oh my God, are you two together?" Saylor's head goes back and forth between us. "I thought you were available," she says to Mike.

"I am, baby," Mike replies and tries to catch Saylor's hand. "Don't listen to her. We hung out months ago, that's it."

"That's it?" I shriek, then lower my voice and address Saylor. "Mike likes to video himself having sex with different girls." I pause. "And he has a very large collection."

A look of shock flashes across Mike's face, as if he can't believe what's coming out of my mouth. Then he turns on the charm. "Saylor, baby, don't listen to her. She's upset because I dumped her."

My jaw drops. "Should I call Paige down here? Or maybe I should just take a survey on campus?"

Saylor stands up. "Thanks, Sophie," she says, then

turns to Mike. "Sorry, you're not worth this kind of drama. And I believe Sophie over you anyway. Later."

Mike turns to me as Saylor takes off with rage in his eyes. "You bitch."

"Grow up," I retort and leave him to fume by himself.

I pass the elevators for the stairs. I'd rather jog up stairs in these heels than spend another minute in the lobby with Mike. I hope that Jean is out. I want to sulk in peace and quiet. I shove open the stairwell door and start jogging up the steps, adrenaline from my confrontation with Mike fueling me. I hear the stairwell door swing open again as I'm rounding the third floor landing and look down to see Mike taking the stairs two at a time.

"Go away, Mike!" I shout behind me and increase my pace.

"I just want you to listen to me, Sophie."

"I don't think so!" My heart is racing so fast I'm afraid I'm going to black out. The stairwells are not used that often and I really do not want to be alone with him. I contemplate exiting onto a lower floor in the hopes of not being stuck alone with Mike, but before I can, I trip over my heels and then I'm falling.

Thirty

Luke's thumb is rubbing back and forth across the back of my hand. It's nice. I love it when he does that. I turn my head towards him and open my eyes.

"Sophie?"

Wait. We're not at Luke's and Luke is not in bed with me. He's sitting next to the bed, wearing scrubs. I blink my eyes as I piece together that I'm in a hospital. I remember fighting with Mike, and then nothing.

"Sophie, how do you feel?" It's Luke. He's standing now, trying to look into my eyes. I shut them.

"It's too bright," I complain. "Where am I?"

"You're at Baldwin Memorial," Luke says, as he reaches over and hits a switch on the wall, dimming the lights. A moment after that the bed is moving, adjusting me so that I'm sitting up.

"Stop, you're annoying me. I'm sleeping."

"You're awake and I need to check your pupils."

"You're a gynecologist."

"I can give you a pelvic when we're done if you like," he replies. "Open your eyes."

I do, and I notice he looks exhausted. He's got a five o'clock shadow and his eyes are red. I love the scrubs though. I've seen him in a lab coat, but never scrubs.

"My head hurts," I tell him.

"I know. Follow my finger," he says, holding it up and moving it left and right, then up and down while I follow with my eyes.

"How long was I asleep?" I ask.

"It's Sunday morning."

"I slept all night?"

"You were unconscious, not asleep, Sophie," he says sharply as he wraps a blood-pressure cuff around my upper arm and inflates it, before unwrapping a stethoscope from around his neck. He places it on my arm and listens as the air is released from the cuff while keeping an eye on his watch. The stethoscope is turning me on so I guess I'm feeling better.

"Why is my ankle wrapped?" I say, catching sight of my leg.

"It's not broken, just sprained," he assures me. "We did an X-ray when you were brought in."

A nurse comes into the room then, moving quickly, her sneakers squeaking across the linoleum floors.

"Good morning, Sophie, we've been waiting for you to wake up. I'm Stacy, I'll be your nurse today. I need to get your vitals."

"I already did," Luke interrupts her, and takes the chart from her hands, writes something in it and hands it back to her.

Stacy looks shocked, and like she might disagree, but decides better of it. "Page me if you need anything, Dr. Miller."

"Bring me the release paperwork, please."

She pauses midstep on her way out the door. "I think Dr. Kallam wanted to see the patient first, Dr. Miller."

"Tell Dr. Kallam I'll have the patient follow up next week."

I look between them, sensing tension, but unsure of what's going on. The nurse leaves without another word and Luke turns his attention back to me.

"What do you remember?"

"I, uh…" I stall. What do I remember? "I remember you left the party with Gina."

"Really, Sophie?" He turns around and walks over to the window and stares at the shitty view from my room for a minute before turning back to me and crossing his arms across his chest. "As fascinating as your childish assumptions are, I'm more interested in how you ended up unconscious in the stairwell of your dorm."

I raise my hand and rub it over the back of my head where it made contact with something—a railing, the floor, I don't know. "He was angry at me," I begin before Luke cuts me off.

"Who was angry?"

"My ex-boyfriend, Mike. He was in the lobby when I got back to the dorm flirting with a girl who lives in my building. I interrupted them and told her what kind of guy he is. He didn't appreciate the interruption."

"Go on," Luke prods.

"I was jogging up the steps, in my heels. That's all I remember."

"Did he touch you?" Luke's face is calm but his voice betrays him.

"No." I shake my head. "No. He was a floor or two behind me. I think I tripped. I should have taken the heels off."

The door swings open then and a tall blonde wearing a

lab coat strides in with a chart in her hands. "Dr. Miller, I hear you're trying to release my patient without me?"

Luke looks like he's had enough of this day and the sun hasn't even finished rising. "Last I checked you reported to me, Dr. Kallam."

"*My* patient," she retorts.

"Kristi," he says warningly.

"Luke," she replies, seemingly unfazed by his ire.

They have a silent battle then, over what I do not know.

"Sophie, how are you feeling?" This is directed at me from Dr. Kallam.

"I think I'm okay," I respond. "I'd really like to leave," I add, in case I have any say in this standoff.

Dr. Kallam shifts her gaze back to Luke and tells him, "One week," on her way out the door.

* * *

We're in Luke's car shortly after that. They wheeled me out in a wheelchair, which I would normally find embarrassing but it turns out I did twist my ankle pretty badly, so I'm not sure I would have been up for a long walk anyway.

"Wait, where are you taking me?" I ask when it's clear Luke is not driving in the direction of campus. It's Sunday. I always go home on Sundays.

"I'm taking you home," he replies testily.

I assume he means his home, but his attitude is not encouraging questions at this point, so I give in and lean back against the headrest and close my eyes. When I open them Luke has already parked the car and he's opening my door to help me out. He scoops me up as soon as the door is closed and carries me to the elevator. I'm in scrubs and an oversized Baldwin Memorial Hospital sweatshirt from Luke's office.

I'd freaked out when Luke had brought me the scrubs to wear home, realizing I must have been wearing Meredith's dress when I was brought in. I'd asked Luke if he'd returned the dress to Meredith and he'd said yes, that he'd called her to the hospital the second I was admitted to pick it up. He was being sarcastic, obviously, but his tone did not brook further conversation.

So here I am, in scrubs. My weekend bag is still upstairs, left there before the gala.

"I'll send for your things," he says as he sets me down on his bed after carrying me from the elevator.

Send for my things? Jesus, he's formal sometimes. "My bag is still here from yesterday," I say, pointing to it on the chair in the corner of the room. "Can you bring it to me, please?" I pull the thin hospital socks off and dig through my bag looking for comfy socks, coming up empty-handed. Luke hands me a pair of his giant tube socks and I grin as I pull them on. Luke's the best. Why was I being such an emotional bitch yesterday?

I should apologize, but when I look up, he's gone.

I riffle through my bag. I have clean clothes, but that makes me realize I want a shower. I slide my legs over the side of the bed and and I'm pulling the scrub top off when Luke reappears with a glass of orange juice.

"Sophie, sit down," he says, handing me the orange juice and directing me to drink it.

"I wanted to take a shower."

"Fine, together," he tells me, pulling the top over my

head. Then he scrubs me down and washes my hair without copping one feel.

"I'm sore all over," I complain.

"You can have two Tylenol," he says, settling me on the couch in the great room.

"Two Tylenol?" I scoff. "I'm dating a doctor and I can't even have the good narcotics?"

He looks at me strangely before replying, "No."

He makes me eat something before Everly and Jeannie show up with a few things from my dorm and my cell phone. Luke says he has calls to make and leaves the three of us to talk without him.

"That man is crazy in love with you, Sophie," Jean says the moment her behind hits the couch, and then fills me in on everything I missed while unconscious.

Apparently I did tumble down the stairs. Mike called for help and Jean was about to get in the ambulance with me when Luke showed up. He tossed her his car keys with instructions for her to meet the ambulance at Baldwin and then hopped in the ambulance still in the tux from the benefit and made them bypass the closer hospital for his. I assume so he could call the shots, like he did this morning with Dr. Kallam.

After they leave I turn my phone on and see the texts from Luke. Worried about me, wondering where I went. The voicemails are worse. He never left the gala, he was walking around looking for me.

I stand up, wanting to find Luke. I walk slowly, finding the kitchen and den empty before moving to the center hallway and calling out for him. I know he didn't leave me here, but where is he?

He appears, coming from the hallway off the front

door, the one that leads to the three empty bedrooms. "What are you doing?" I ask him, nodding toward the hallway he just came from with a tilt of my head.

"Thinking," he replies, and shrugs, hands in his pockets. He looks me in the eye then and pauses. "Anything you're thinking about?"

"Um, yeah. I wanted to apologize." Shit, this is hard. "I don't know why I assumed that you left with Gina. It was really childish of me to leave and not answer your call. I'm sorry."

He nods. "Okay."

"Okay?"

"Yes, okay. Anything else?"

"No." I shake my head.

He picks me up then and carries me to bed to rest. He lies next to me and rubs my back while I drift in and out.

* * *

There's no class on Monday. School is closed for Martin Luther King Day. The extra day off is great—I don't think I could have managed campus.

"I'm going to class today," I tell him Tuesday morning. "And you're going to work."

"Am I?" he asks, sipping a cup of coffee and leaning against the island in the kitchen.

"Yes." I take in his appearance. He is dressed for work, so he must be planning on going. "I'm sure women are ovulating and in need of your services."

"I'm sure," he responds dryly.

"You're not going to fight me about leaving the house today?"

"No, I'm going to drive you to class myself."

Huh, that was easier than I thought.

"You will stay on campus and I will pick you up at the end of the day." He pauses. "Got it?"

"Got it, big daddy."

"Cute. Are you ready to leave?"

He drops me off at the door of the Hymer building and picks me up at the campus library at the end of the day.

He opens the passenger door of an SUV and I pause, staring at the car. It's a huge Land Rover. "You bought a new car today?" I question as I slide in. He closes the door and walks around to the driver's side.

"I did."

"Is this supposed to make me feel safer than the Mercedes?"

He glances at me. "No, not particularly."

"You just decided today was the day for a new car?" I ask.

"The Mercedes wasn't very practical."

Practical? For what? "Did you save it for me?" I tease.

"Do you want to be driving a two-seater car, Sophie?" He looks like this concerns him.

"I'm joking, relax," I laugh. "My grandparents are giving me their old Honda for graduation. I won't be able to afford an apartment and a car payment."

"Right." He pauses as he turns the car on. "Right."

We drive to Rittenhouse Square in silence and Luke leads me straight into the kitchen when we arrive. "Mrs. Geiger left us dinner," he says, pulling open the warming drawers under the island countertop. "Sit," he tells me and slides a plate of lasagna in front of me.

I slump into one of the chairs at the island. "I'm exhausted," I admit.

"It'll pass," Luke says. He doesn't sit, instead leaning against the opposite counter with his plate, watching me.

Is he just going to watch me eat? He's been so weird the last few days.

His phone rings and he answers it as I finish eating. It's a work call and he heads into his den to finish it as I place my plate in the dishwasher and head to his bedroom to grab my cell phone charger. I think I left it plugged in next to the bed. I grab it and turn around to take it to the television room but I stop short as I pass the empty closet closest to the bedroom door, because it's no longer empty.

There are two walk-in closets in this room. An empty one near the door and a second across from the bathroom filled with Luke's things. But now the empty one is filled with my things. I walk inside and look around. It's the entire contents of my dorm room. It doesn't even fill the closet, that's how little I own. But it's all here. My textbooks are stacked neatly on a shelf probably meant for sweaters. My meager wardrobe is hanging on wooden hangers, my shoes neatly lined up in a row underneath. My cosmetics and shower caddy are on another shelf.

Has he... moved me in with him? What the ever-loving hell? Who does that? Someone took all my stuff and moved it into Luke's house without my consent. What did he say the other day? *I'll send for your things?* Was that asking me to move in? I'm so stunned I don't know what to do next. I exit the bedroom and walk down the hall to his office and stop just inside the doorway and stare at him. He's off the phone now, typing on his laptop. He pauses when I don't say anything.

"Yes?" he prods.

"Do I live here now?" I ask him, radiating attitude. "Do I get a key too? Or will you be driving me to school and picking me up every day like a child?" Jesus, transportation. How does he expect me to get to and from school every day? "Wait, are you really thinking you're going to drive me to school?"

"For the time being, yes, I was thinking exactly that." He closes the laptop and leans back in his chair.

"Did we discuss this while I was unconscious? Because I don't remember having a conversation about moving in with you."

Luke rubs his bottom lip with his thumb before answering. "Logistically I thought my place made the most sense."

Logistically? Sense? Nothing he's saying makes any sense. "Why is Gina your patient?" I ask. If he wants to have a crazy talk, let's do it.

"She's not," he says, opening his laptop back up. "Not any longer."

"But she was," I say and I know my voice is not neutral.

"You know that I can't confirm that due to doctor-patient confidentiality, but since you seem to already know, and in the interest of ending this conversation, yes, she was my patient. And she is not anymore."

"But why?" I'm confused. "Why was she ever, Luke?"

He sighs and rubs a hand across his face. "We have a history, Sophie. I felt like I owed it to her to help, but I don't anymore." He looks at me. "Is that enough?"

I don't know, but I'm tired, so honestly, I give up on this fight or whatever it is and go to bed.

Thirty-One

Luke insists on driving me to and from class for the rest of the week. I fear for the future population of Philadelphia with the amount of work he must be missing.

On Sunday I wake up in Luke's bed, same as the rest of the week. It's nice being here. Showering in Luke's giant walk-in shower every morning instead of the questionable dorm showers doesn't suck, that's for sure.

I'm alone in bed this morning, which isn't unusual. Luke hits the gym before I'm awake most days. I stretch under the covers. The mattress quality at Luke's is a world away from dorm life too.

I'm still not sure what I'm doing here. Have I moved in? It would be nice to be asked. Is it permanent?

I stare at the view of Philadelphia from the bed while I think.

Luke's been weird all week. It's sweet, actually. I think he's worried about me, but I'm fine. I don't have any lasting effects from the concussion and my ankle is okay.

He hasn't touched me all week, sexually. Maybe I should initiate? Let him know I'm fine? I've never had to initiate before though, not really. I mean hell, usually smiling can be perceived as an invitation with Luke.

"You're awake," Luke says from the bedroom doorway.

I didn't hear him come in. He's got a towel thrown over his shoulder, his hair tousled from his workout.

"Come back to bed." I pat the bed with my hand.

He walks to the bed and, bracing his weight on his hands, leans in and kisses me. "I'm sweaty. Take a shower with me and we'll go out for breakfast."

Dammit, does he not want to have sex with me? Breakfast sounds like a great idea though. "I want waffles."

"I know you do," he says, pulling the covers off of me.

"And an omelet."

He extends a hand to pull me from the bed.

"Bacon too," I add. "I want all the food, actually."

"We'll order four breakfasts and pretend people are joining us."

"Are you teasing me?" I'm detecting a smirk on his face.

"Never. We'll go to the buffet at Lacroix. They have all the food, I promise."

A buffet? Hell, yes. I bounce out of bed and dash past Luke for the shower.

Luke is ready before me, as he insists I cannot leave the house with wet hair. I'm dressed and sitting on top of the bathroom vanity, hair dryer in hand while Luke stands in the bathroom door fastening his watch to his wrist.

"Almost dry," I tell him. "Can you bring me my purse, please?"

He nods and retrieves it from the floor of my closet and sets it on the counter. I click off the dryer, satisfied the moisture level of my hair will pass inspection, and dig through my purse. I brush some bronzer across my face and apply mascara before coating my lips in pumpkin spice lip balm. Then I pop out today's birth control pill from the packet and pop it into my mouth while filling a glass of water.

"What are you doing, Sophie?" Luke is suddenly beside me, digging into my purse.

"Relax, I'm ready." I didn't take that long. He has no appreciation for how fast I am.

"With these, Sophie," he says, holding up my birth control pills. "What are you doing with these?" He looks pissed.

I stare at the pack in his hand. I haven't missed any, I take them every morning. "I always take them in the morning, Luke, same time every day." I shrug. "Well, within an hour or two."

He stares at me for a second before tossing the pills onto the counter. The pack whips across the surface before hitting the wall and ricocheting into the sink. He turns around and walks to the bathroom door, gripping the door frame for a second before turning back to face me.

"Sophie, you're pregnant."

Thirty-Two

There's dead silence then. I feel a moment of absolute nothing before my mind starts racing at warp speed. We stare at each other, Luke watching my reaction, my face giving away a myriad of feelings all at once.

"What?"

He doesn't respond, just keeps watching me.

"I'm not." I shake my head. "I take my pills every day. Every single day. I haven't been on any antibiotics." I shake my head again. "No, no, I'm not, Luke."

He looks sad as he leans against the bathroom doorway. "We did a blood test before taking a CT scan of your head while you were in the hospital. And we confirmed it with an ultrasound."

"You've known this for a week?" I'm feeling semi-hysterical right now and I'm sure I sound it.

"I thought you must know," he says slowly, "and I wanted to give you the chance to tell me yourself."

I grab my purse and push past him in the doorway on my way to my closet. I grab a bag and start tossing things into it randomly.

"What are you doing, Sophie?" Luke is blocking the door to the closet, watching me.

"I'm leaving," I tell him. I'm trying so hard not to cry,

tears are threatening to fall and I blink my eyes trying to stop them. "I'm going home, where I'm not pregnant." God, that doesn't even make sense. I sling the bag over my shoulder and turn to face him in the doorway, but I can't meet his eyes. I have to get out of here before I lose it. "Please move, Luke," I say, staring at his chest.

There's a pause and then he steps back and I bolt past him.

"Sophie," he calls out after me, but I don't stop and the front door slams behind me as I flee.

I'm not pregnant. He doesn't know everything. I need to pee on a stick. I am not pregnant. These thoughts bounce around my head as I take the elevator to the lobby and refuse the town car the doorman tries to place me in. I take off down 18th Street. There's a CVS around the corner on Chestnut. I hustle down the sidewalk, intent on getting a pregnancy test.

I walk around CVS in a daze. Where are the pregnancy tests? I've never needed one before. I find them in the feminine care aisle, tampons and pregnancy tests all in one spot. Seems ironic since you only need one or the other.

Okay, pregnancy tests. I scan the row. Why are there choices? Will one choice make me less pregnant? Don't they all do the same thing? I feel panicky, I need to get out of here, but which test do I choose? I take three of them and walk to the checkout.

The cashier scans them and asks if I want a bag. Why wouldn't I want a bag? Am I supposed to take them into the back room and pee on them here? I stare at her name tag. Holly. Maybe I'm pregnant with a girl and we'll name her Holly. Holly Miller. I lose the battle with the tears then and they streak down my face. I don't want a baby named Holly.

"So I'll just put these in a bag then," the cashier says as I swipe my card. "With your receipt," she adds, as if asking me if I would like the receipt in the bag will push me over the edge. I'm clearly not capable of answering the tough questions right now.

I grab the bag and walk down Chestnut in the direction of campus. I have no idea what I'm doing. There's a Dunkin' Donuts ahead on my right and I push the door open and walk in.

I stand staring at the menu board until someone behind me asks if I'm in line. I shake my head and tell them to go ahead, then skip the line altogether and lock myself into the bathroom. I open all the boxes and skip the directions. Pee on the stick, wait. Look for a plus sign or double lines, got it. I finish and shove them all into one box and then into my purse and exit the bathroom.

I stare at the menu board again. I should have a donut. That's the normal thing to do while waiting for a pregnancy test, right? Has it been three minutes? The pregnancy tests are in my bag, waiting, while I look at donuts. Cream-filled? Jelly? Oh, look, they have heart-shaped donuts for Valentine's Day.

What kind of idiot has to be told they're pregnant by their boyfriend? I keep picturing Luke's face as I order two jelly-filled donuts and one of the heart-shaped ones with pink frosting. I add an orange juice. The smell of the coffee is almost ruining my desire for the donuts.

I probably can't have coffee anymore anyway. Stupid baby. I slide the orange juice in my coat pocket and continue walking down Chestnut while I shove a jelly donut in my mouth.

I walk and walk and walk. I reach the Schuylkill and realize I can cross the bridge on foot. Might as well just walk all the way home. Luke's penthouse condo is ridiculously close to my dorm room really. Forty-five minutes on foot, tops, less than fifteen by car. But we're worlds apart, aren't we?

He looked so disappointed when he said I was pregnant. Oh, God. I want to throw up, and not because of hormones. How many times did he lecture me about birth control? I think back to the very beginning, in the clinic when I was his patient. Using condoms just because I threw up a couple of times when I was hungover, the birth control refills that were handed to me.

I've become my mother, but worse. My father didn't care he was being used to father children he had no interest in. Luke cares.

I dump the empty orange juice bottle into a trash can and yank open my purse and dump the pregnancy tests as well. I don't need them. It's not like Luke of all people doesn't know what he's doing. My denial is quickly fading, replaced by anger. This is not what I had planned.

I turn right onto Spruce and see Luke leaning against his big stupid SUV in front of Jacobsen Hall. We make eye contact briefly as I approach and he nods but doesn't attempt to talk to me. I cannot believe he knocked me up. Jerk.

I push open the door of my dorm room and walk in on Jean and Jonathan having sex. Can this day get any worse? I should count my blessings at this point, at least there were no toys involved this time. I slump against the wall across from our door and slide down to the floor in a heap. I have one donut left, the heart-shaped one covered in pink frosting. There are heart-shaped sprinkles on top too, I notice as I shove it in my mouth.

The door opens and Jonathan appears with Jean right behind him.

"Sophie, what are you doing here?" Jean asks, concern on her face.

"Eating a donut." I hold up the remaining half as evidence.

They look at each other for a moment and then Jonathan helps me off the floor while Jean holds the door open. Once I'm on my feet Jonathan takes off and I flop across my old bed.

"What's going on, Sophie? I thought you were staying with Luke?"

"I'm"—I sigh—"pregnant."

"Oh." Jean looks surprised. "Oh, wow." She's quiet for a moment. "Luke didn't take it well?"

"He's the one who told me."

"He knew before you did?" she asks incredulously.

"I'm an idiot," I reply, blowing hair off my face.

"No, Sophie, no, you're not. What's going on?"

I fill her in and she listens patiently. She rubs my back while I cry and lets me talk and vent all afternoon. All week really. And she lends me clothing, since Luke moved all of my things into his house.

Luke calls, and I send him to voicemail. I'm not ready to talk to him. I'm not ready for any of this.

Thirty-Three

"Holy shit. Pregnant?" Everly looks horrified. She's staring at my stomach like she suspects baby cooties are airborne.

"It's not contagious, Everly."

"I know that," she responds unconvincingly while running a hand across her flat stomach. She hops up on the back counter and stares at me while swinging her feet. "Have you told Luke? How'd he take it? Are you gonna HEA?"

"Are we going to what?"

Everly rolls her eyes at me. "HEA. Are you going to get married, have the baby and live happily ever after?"

"I don't know." I shake my head.

"Well, how did he react when you told him? He's really old, he might want a kid," she offers.

"He told me, actually."

Everly stops swinging her legs. "How? Were you playing some kinky pregnancy test game? Please say yes," she pleads.

"Uh, no." I point to my head. "Concussion? Hospital? Remember?"

"Oh, right," she says, deflating.

"Enough about me. What's new with Professor

Camden?"

Everly freezes for a brief second then shrugs. "Nothing. And if you think I'm done talking about the chicken nugget in your uterus, you're mistaken."

I ignore her and move to assist a customer.

"So, what's your plan?" Everly asks when I'm done.

"It's been three days, Everly, I'm supposed to have a plan?"

Everly looks at me like I'm crazy. "Yeah, you're Sophie. You probably had a plan within three hours."

I slump against the counter. "I had planned to graduate without a pregnancy, so maybe planning isn't all it's cracked up to be."

Everly just waves her hand for me to continue.

"I think I can afford a one-bedroom in a decent area as long as I find a full-time position by graduation."

"You can afford a three-bedroom and a pony with the amount of child support Luke will be paying."

"No." I shake my head. "No, I don't want his money. I'm not my mother." The back of my eyes burn and I will myself not to cry.

Everly hops off the counter and hugs me. "I know, bitch. I know," she says, rubbing my back. Only Everly can call me a bitch at a moment like this and make it comforting. "Sophie, you're the most conscientious person I know. No one will think you got pregnant on purpose."

I spot a shiny new Land Rover parking out front as I pull away from Everly. I can't believe he's stopping in for his Tuesday morning coffee run like nothing has happened. I duck into the back and leave Everly to deal with him, busying myself unpacking a shipment of paper cups.

I don't stop until Everly appears, leaning against the door jamb. "You're so stupid," she says in way of greeting.

"I know," I agree, slumping.

"No, dumbass, about Luke." She points her thumb in the direction of the street. "He traded in a sports car for an SUV."

"Everly, I don't want his money. He can buy three cars for all I care."

"I cannot believe you're the smart one," she mutters. "First of all, that's a luxury Land Rover, not a car. And secondly, it's a *Land Rover*, Sophie—that's the equivalent to a minivan for Luke. Jesus, he probably has a baby name site bookmarked on his laptop. You two are gross," she finishes and walks back into the shop.

I chew on my bottom lip while I think about what Everly is saying.

"He asked about you," she calls out as she walks away.

* * *

The next two days pass in a blur. I attend class, study and send out resumes. Boyd leaves me several messages about meeting to talk, but my energy level is so low all I've managed to do is text him back. Being an incubator is exhausting.

I'm confused. Everly and Jean haven't been with Luke these last few months. They haven't heard the reminders about taking my pill at the same time every day, the refills being handed to me. The inquiries about my period. I don't think Luke wants a baby. At least not this second, or maybe just not with me.

I'm back at Grind Me on Thursday working when I look up to find Boyd across the counter from me.

"Hey, Boyd," I greet him.

"You've been ignoring my calls, little sister." He smiles as he says it.

"I'm sorry." I pause. "I've had a lot going on."

"Yeah. I remember college life. I'm sure you've got better things to do than return family phone calls."

"I wish it were that simple." I groan.

Boyd frowns. "Listen," he says, tapping an envelope I'm only now noticing on the counter. "I have to leave town for a bit for work, and I wanted to take care of this before I left. Can you take a break? Or we can meet after your shift?"

We sit in a corner booth and Boyd slides the envelope across to me.

"What is this?" I ask, holding it between my fingertips.

"Your inheritance."

"What?" I drop the envelope on the table in alarm.

"Your inheritance," he repeats. "From our father."

"That's yours, Boyd." I shake my head. "I don't want it."

Boyd shakes his head at me and runs a hand over his jaw. "He meant for you to have that, Sophie."

I barely refrain from snorting. "He never even bothered to meet me."

"I talked to my mom," Boyd says. "She knew."

I slump in the booth. I'm not sure if that's better or worse. I'd hoped she was oblivious to the fact that her husband cheated on her. But why did I wish that? So I didn't have to feel guilty on my mother's behalf? How stupid.

"I'm sorry, Sophie."

Wait, what? "Why are you sorry? I'm the one who should be apologizing to you."

Boyd laughs. "Why?"

"My mom had no business messing around with your dad. He was married."

Boyd tilts his head and gazes at me for a minute. "Is that what you've been carrying around in your head these last few months? Sophie, we have nothing to do with anything that happened over twenty years ago between our parents. And if either of us should feel guilty for our parents' actions, it's me, not you. Your mom was barely an adult, yet as far as I can tell, she's the only one who responded like an adult to a bad situation."

"What do you mean?" I've never really looked at my mom that way before.

"My mom knew about the affair, Sophie. And she lived in fear, not of losing our dad, but of having her sham of a marriage exposed. She didn't want to end up on the covers of the newspapers as yet another scorned political wife."

"Can't say I blame her, Boyd."

He ignores me and continues. "When she learned your mom was pregnant she threatened to cut off our father's campaign funding if he didn't end it with her. Discreetly. Our father had a decent net worth by the time he passed," he says, nodding to the envelope, "but my mother's family has the real money. The kind of money you need to win a campaign."

"So he chose his political career," I fill in.

Boyd nods. "But I dug around some more. He never

JANA ASTON

meant to write you out completely. Not financially at least. You"—he nods to the envelope—"were supposed to receive that when you turned eighteen."

I center the envelope on the table in front of me. "Why didn't I?" I ask, looking up at Boyd.

"My mother," he answers with a grimace. "She had it buried. She knew with our father's death that no one else knew about you. She didn't count on a paper trail that would come back to haunt her."

I blow the air out of my lungs. "I'm a mess, Boyd. I'm pregnant," I blurt out and continue in a rush. "I'm pregnant. I'm just like my mother. I'm repeating the cycle! I'm gonna have a baby just like me. And half this baby's family will pretend it doesn't exist."

Boyd leans back in the booth and tilts his head. "Are you pregnant with a married senatorial candidate's baby?"

"No. Don't be ridiculous. Luke's the only affair I've had. The baby is Luke's."

"Luke's married?"

"No!"

Boyd shakes his head. "Do we need to have a come-to-Jesus moment, little sister? How are you anything like our father and your mother?" Boyd asks, leaning his elbows on the table top.

"Because it wasn't planned, Boyd. Luke doesn't want a baby. And his family hates me."

"Is that what Luke said?" Boyd scowls. "Is that what he said when you told him?"

"Well, no. He knew before I did." Boyd's eyebrows rise at this. "And technically he's the one who told me."

"And then he offered to set up a trust fund for the baby's eighteenth birthday and kicked you out?"

"No! Then I left before he had the chance."

"Oh."

"I just, I feel like a burden. He didn't ask for this."

"Neither did you, Sophie. But you got in this together and you haven't even given him the courtesy of discussing it like the adults you both are."

Hmm. He has a point.

"You don't need Luke, Sophie. If he's not interested in participating in this baby's life, you've got plenty of options in that envelope right in front of you, and you're graduating in a couple of months. You don't need anyone to take care of you. And no one is running you off except for you. Talk to Luke."

Thirty-Four

The cab drops me off outside the main entrance at Baldwin Memorial. The electronic doors whoosh open before me and I pause for a moment on the sidewalk. This is it. I need to talk to Luke and find out exactly what he's thinking. I'm having a baby, his baby. It wasn't in my plans, but it's happening all the same.

I take a deep breath. The sky is clear today, the air crisp with the promise of spring around the corner. It occurs to me how much is about to change. Graduation is in May, I'll be moving off campus, and sometime this fall I'll be a mother. I falter for a second on that thought. I'm going to be a mother—not someday, but this year—and the idea terrifies me.

I will be leaving a hospital, maybe this one, with a newborn baby thrust into my arms. I know I won't be a terrible mother, but what if I'm not a good one? What if I'm just passable at it? What if it doesn't come naturally to me and I make questionable parenting choices? What if I have to do this all alone?

The doors whoosh again and I take in a gulp of fresh air and walk inside. I bypass the welcome desk and head straight for the elevators, intent on my destination. The energy inside the hospital is so different from outside. It's sterile, sure, but palpable. It occurs to me as I hit the call button that I don't know for certain that Luke is here. I'm usually in class on Friday afternoons. Luke is here most of the time, as far as I can tell.

I exit the elevator on Luke's floor and make my way to his office, the smell of antiseptic stinging my nose.

"Sophie!"

The doctor from my stay here a couple of weeks ago approaches. "Sophie," she repeats. "I'm Dr. Kallam. I treated you when you were here," she says, searching my face for recognition. "Are you here to see me or Luke?"

Oh, right, she wanted to see me for a followup.

"Yes, I remember you, Dr. Kallam. I'm here to see Luke, but I guess I need to make an appointment with you? I have no idea what I'm doing," I find myself confessing, touching my stomach. Am I already messing this up? "I…" I pause. "Is it okay?" I look at Dr. Kallam for reassurance. "I'm not supposed to be doing anything special yet, am I?"

Dr. Kallam smiles at me. She's a beautiful woman, about Luke's age. I feel a twinge of annoyance that Luke is surrounded by so many attractive women at work, all more competent than me in this baby business.

"It's still early, Sophie. I'd like you to start a prenatal vitamin, cut out any alcohol and caffeine and get plenty of rest. That's enough for now and you'll need to start regular appointments with your primary OBGYN."

I shake my head. "I don't have one."

"You can make an appointment with my office or Luke can provide you a list to choose from. I'm surprised he didn't explain this to you." Dr. Kallam tucks a piece of perfectly curled hair behind her left ear and gazes at me questioningly.

"We haven't talked much," I offer.

She nods. "He's with a patient right now. I'll let you into his office. I'm sorry I allowed you to leave without us speaking, but Luke was very insistent that you have the opportunity to tell him yourself."

"I didn't know," I tell her as she unlocks his door and we sit in the chairs across from Luke's desk. "I had no idea. I've taken my birth control religiously. He thought I knew?" I look to Dr. Kallam for confirmation.

She pauses then nods. "It was really important to him to hear it from you."

"Why? He's made a career out of telling women they're pregnant."

"He has." Dr. Kallam smiles at my description of his work. "I imagine he didn't want you to feel pressured."

"He wanted me to decide if I would keep it without his influence?"

She nods slightly before speaking. "I've been friends with Luke for a long time," she says before trailing off, leaving me to fill in the blanks.

She gets a page then and stands. "I've got to run, Sophie. Please call my office and get on my schedule or let me know if you need a referral."

She leaves, a whiff of her perfume lingering behind her as the door shuts, and I'm left alone in Luke's office. I tap my fingers on the chair edge and stare at the low bookcases along the wall. Above them is a corkboard running the length of the wall filled with pictures of babies, and upon closer inspection, what looks like thank-you letters from new parents. Gah, I know nothing about babies. I stare at the pictures for a moment. They're so small. How does one even dress something that small? I examine the shelves underneath looking for a baby manual of some kind. It's mainly medical journals but I locate a few copies of *What to Expect When You're Expecting*. They look new, as if Luke keeps them for potentially overwhelmed pregnant patients. He probably doesn't need to read any of this himself, having memorized it in medical school. At least one of us has a clue.

I slide a copy off the shelf and move around to Luke's chair so I can lay the book flat on his desk. Why is this book so big? I'm overwhelmed as I turn to the first page and even more so by the time I reach page twenty. I need to take notes. I glance around Luke's desk for something to write on and, coming up empty, open the desk drawer.

My eyes take in the contents, but my brain is on slow motion trying to process what I'm seeing when there's a tap on the door followed by Gina breezing in like she's entitled. I close the drawer and watch as the smile she had reserved for Luke falls off her face.

"Snooping in Luke's office, Sophie? Have a little class, would you?"

Oh, good, we're going to hit the ground running today. "May I help you with something, Gina? Like the number to a dating service? I'm sure one of them specializes in finding matches for trolls."

"Cute, but save it for yourself. I have Luke." Her face is smug.

"You don't." I shake my head. "You might have once, but you most definitely do not have him now. Because I do, and I'm not giving him up."

Her eyes land on the book open facedown on the desk

and I can see a hiccup of terror cross her face. "You're pregnant?" She's stunned. "I can't believe Luke would let this happen, he's so careful."

I want to vomit into Luke's trash can at the knowledge that she knows anything about Luke, much less his proficiency at birth control, but suddenly things start falling into place.

"You had an abortion, didn't you? When you dated Luke, you had an abortion." I don't even need her to confirm it. Everything finally adds up.

"Luke doesn't want children, Sophie," Gina spits. "He's focused on his career, he doesn't have the time or desire for children to slow him down. He's going to dump you and you're going to be fat and alone."

I know she's lying. There's a Wall of Baby with cherubic little faces and handwritten thank-yous from their parents that prove she is lying. The man made a career out of helping women become mothers, the pictures proudly documenting his success. I don't think for a second that he doesn't want that for himself. Yet her words sting, like shrapnel. Even lying words are hurtful.

"I think," I say slowly, "you're a liar. I think Luke is careful with contraception because some troll from his past had an abortion he didn't want. I think Luke respects me and wanted the timing to be my choice. And finally, Gina, I know Luke wants this baby. Our baby. It's over, Gina. This pathetic attempt of yours to guilt Luke about a decision you made by having him treat you for infertility is over. Do you even have infertility issues or was it all a ploy to spend time with him?" I shake my head. "You need psychological help, not a gynecologist. Now get the hell out of Luke's office and my life."

The door slams behind her and I dive back into the desk drawer, running my hand over the contents. I pull one out and run my fingers across the Christmas fabric. Christmas was a month ago—Luke didn't know I was pregnant until two weeks ago. I pull the drawer open farther and teeny-tiny turkeys peer up at me. Thanksgiving was two months ago. He's been collecting a stash of adorable baby socks for at least two months. The kind of socks I'd wear in miniature form. There's a pink pair, covered in red hearts. Another pair covered in little peanut butter and jelly sandwiches. The tiny red and white striped elf socks still in my hands.

That hot son of a bitch wants me to have his baby.

I don't feel duped. I believe what I told Gina. I think he did want the timing to be my choice. I place the socks back in the drawer and slide it shut with a thump.

I look at the six-hundred-page book in front of me and, feeling overwhelmed by everything I don't know, snap it shut and place it back on the shelf. Returning to Luke's chair, I tuck my feet up beside me and wrap my arms around my bent knees.

I'm wondering how much longer I'll be able to sit like this before my stomach prevents such a configuration when Luke walks in. He pauses with his hand on the doorknob, taking me in, sitting behind his desk.

"Sophie," he says, looking relieved to see me, yet wary at the same time. He shuts the door behind him with a click and takes a seat across from me.

"You bought a car that will accommodate car seats?"

"Yes," he replies, his face giving away nothing at my random conversation starter. I expected some kind of denial, so I'm not sure what to do with this.

"You got a baby car before telling me"—I point to myself—"that we're having a baby. That's wrong, don't you think?" I say with a hint of ire. "You're ridiculous. We won't even need it for another eight months."

He smiles then, the biggest smile I think I've ever seen on this face. "Seven, actually."

I pause and drop my hand. I don't even know how pregnant I am. I shake my head at him and turn my gaze away from him as Luke moves around to sit on the edge of the desk in front of me.

"Why are you mad?" he asks, caressing my cheek with his thumb. "I know it's scary, Sophie, but everything's going to be fine. Perfect, even."

"You're laughing at me," I protest.

"I'm not." He shakes his head to emphasize it.

"Then why are you smiling?"

"Because you said we're having a baby."

"Well, yeah," I answer, confused. "You already knew that."

"I knew you were pregnant." He pauses, searching my eyes. "I didn't know if you'd want it."

"I do want it. But I'm scared. This isn't what I'd planned."

"I know you have plans that don't include a baby just yet, and I'm sorry I put you in this position. But if this is what you want, we can make it work." He stops and searches my face again. "I want it, Sophie. You, the baby, all of it."

I nod. "We'll figure it out."

"Together?"

He holds out his hand and I take it.

Epilogue

Luke

Sophie doesn't know it, but today is our fifth anniversary. Five years ago today I took a wrong turn that changed my life. There was construction on Walnut. I detoured and missed my normal stop at Starbucks. I spotted Grind Me and stopped on a whim, desperate for a jolt of caffeine before the clinic.

I had no reason to go back the next week. Or the week after that. Weeks of detours for no reason other than a glance at a barista named Sophie. I had to finish the coffee in my damn car every day since I wasn't about to walk into a student clinic holding a cup stamped Grind Me.

I never intended to start up anything with her. I knew she was young. I assumed she was a grad student at the very least, but that was still too young for me. It was nothing more than a harmless ego boost at first - watching her pupils dilate when I spoke, her cheeks flush when she handed me coffee. Seeing her eyes follow me in the reflection of the glass every morning as I strode out of the cafe.

Slowly I began to question, Why not her? I could take

her out to dinner. Fuck her. Get her out of my system. But hell, she looked like the kind of girl who'd need to be called the next day. She looked like the kind of girl who had baby names picked out and would practice writing Mrs. Miller on scraps of paper. She looked *terrifying*.

But I didn't have any idea what terrifying actually felt like until I realized that I was the one who wanted all those things, and I wasn't sure she did. That maybe the past was repeating itself. That maybe Sophie might be more interested in a career than a husband and children, with no faith that she could have *both*.

I glance at her, sleeping next to me. She's stirring with the morning sun filtering in. We don't have long before the girls will be awake and the day begins. I reach over and trace kisses down her jaw to her chest.

"Mmm, good morning to you too, Dr. Miller. Tell me you locked the door?" she pleads.

I release a nipple from my teeth before replying. "Locked, and they're both still asleep." I part her legs and move between them as I kiss her stomach. "Based on the time we should have at least twenty minutes."

She laughs. "Remember when we had all day?"

"I do." I grin at her.

"I miss the marathons, but I do enjoy seeing how creative you can be on a deadline."

"Do you?" I ask and drop her ankles over my shoulders.

"Uh-huh."

"I enjoy it when you visit me at work after dropping the girls off at the hospital daycare."

"Do you think we're bad parents? Are the other parents using daycare to slip in a middle-of-the-day fuck?"

"If they're not, they should be."

"It was one thing when they couldn't walk, but they're little terrors now."

I pause and raise my head. "You don't want another one?"

"We have two!" she exclaims. "Under five! I just got Christine off to pre-school and I finally have Alessandra out of diapers."

"Well, maybe you'll change your mind?" I raise an eyebrow at her.

"Wait a minute." She sits up and scoots away from me. "Wait, wait, wait." She eyes me, scowling. "Do you think I'm pregnant now?"

"You're three days late."

"You're three days annoying."

"I love the way your insults don't even make sense when you're flustered." I reach for her calf to pull her back to me, but she dodges me and grabs her phone from the nightstand.

I wait patiently while she thumbs through looking for her period-tracker app.

"How do you do that?" She scowls. "You don't even have the app!"

"Pregnancy tests under the sink," I call out as she stomps off to the bathroom. "I can get a blood draw this week when you stop in for office sex."

"Thanks, babe, that's convenient," she replies sarcastically, and I just laugh.

I hear the stick hit the trash can before she appears from the bathroom with a sigh she doesn't mean. I smile and crook my finger, beckoning her back to bed to finish what we started.

Something thumps against the bedroom door and the handle shakes back and forth. "Mommy?"

She sags. "There goes morning sex. For the next decade."

"Just a minute," I call out to whichever kid is in the hallway. "You," I say to her, "get back in bed. Give me five minutes, I'll set them up with a snack and a Disney movie and be right back."

She bites back a smirk. "You're going to distract our children with a movie so we can have sex? You're so wrong."

Acknowledgements

Julie Huss,
Thank you for refusing to write the gynecologist erotica I kept asking for and telling me to go write it myself. Fine! I will! Um… okay. How do I use scrivener? How much is editing? Can you make me a cover? A pink one. XXOO,heart, heart, flower.

Kristi Carol,
Thank you for reading this from the very beginning in little bits & pieces, which is the worst way to read a book. Yet you kept reading it & kept asking for more, which means more to me than you'll ever know.

Beverly Tubb,
Thank you for reading the first draft and loving it at a time I was ready to shelve the entire thing. Your repeated insistence that it was good and that you loved it may have very well been the difference between hitting the publish button versus the trash button.

Michelle New,
First, thank you for being you. Steady and drama free, always. Second, your graphics blow me away. Seeing *my*

book through your graphic eyes? Just, wow. Thank you.

Is anyone still reading this? Holy shit. **THANK YOU.** I never set out to write a book. Like, ever. I don't have a notebook filled with short stories from my childhood. I didn't take a class. I just decided to do it one day. I'm not saying it was easy, or that I didn't work really hard on it. Because it wasn't & I did. I'd estimate that 90% of this book was written by hand, a sentence squeezed in a moment here and a minute there throughout days, then months. I spent weekends typing it then eventually sent it off for professional editing. Then a second round of professional editing. So while I didn't have much of a game plan going in, I did my best to create a satisfying story that was free of grammatical errors and typos. If you enjoyed it, thank you. I know your time is valuable & I appreciate that you spent some it reading Wrong.

If you read this because you know me as Jana Aston, Julie Huss' assistant, thanks for giving me a chance. Our styles & stories could not be more different. If you're hoping my life plan is to become an author & leave my assistant days behind me, sorry you're **WRONG**. You'll have to crowbar me out of that role. I have a front row seat to the genius that is JA Huss. I get to talk with her about upcoming books. Months before a title's even been announced, I get to hear about it. And she lets me argue with her about shit like hating the names she's picked out (Did you know Rory Shrike's name was going to be Sugar? Sugar Shrike? Assistant fit was thrown.) Or the mental state of her characters, (Apparently James is crazy, according to her. Uh, no. James is perfect, amiright?) The point is, if you were hoping that position was about to open up, sorrynotsorry.

If you think you spotted your name inside the book, you probably did. Ali **Hymer**, **Alessandra** Torre, Amber **Jacobsen**, Amber **Gladson,** Ashley **Blackwell**, Beverly Tubb, **Bella Love**, **Brandee** Price, Chelsea **Holguin**, Christy **Baldwin**, **Christine** Reiss, **Heidi** Tieman, **Holly** Brama, Jennifer **Mirabelli**, **Jean** Siska, Jessica **Frider**, **Julie** Huss, **June** Luu, **Kaylee** Marie, **Katie** Terranova, **Kara** Hummel, Krista Lohss **Davis**, **Kristi Kallam**, **Laura** Moore Helseth, **Leah** Davis, Lindsey **Miller**, **Marie** Jocke, Michelle **New**, Misty Crook **McElroy,** Nicole **Alexander**, **Meredith** Dixon, Michelle **Tan**, Nicole **Tetrev**, **Paige** Nero Gast, Reanell **Tisdale**, Sandra **Stroh**, Sarah **Geiger**, **Sarah** Piechuta, **Shay** Savage, **Stacy** Bono, Tami **Estes**, Tiffany **Halliday**, Tiffany **Hollett**, Tiffany **Saylor**, Trisha **Hudson**, Veronica **LaRoche.** Thank you for touching my life during the writing of this book.

Is this the part where I'm supposed to tell you about my future plans? I…. don't know. Everly has a story. I'd like to think I will tell it to you, but this book releasing thing is exhausting. I'd really like to tell it to you though, because Everly's story is not quite what you think.

About Jana

Jana Aston loves to read sexy romance novels, especially if they involve an alpha CEO. WRONG is her first novel.

After writing her debut novel, she quit her super boring day job to whip up her second novel, RIGHT. She's hoping that was not a stupid idea.

In her defense, it was a really boring job.

Newsletter

If you enjoyed this book, please consider signing up for my newsletter at www.janaaston.com. It is the only way that I can reach you directly and let you know when I have a new book available.

I do not sell my newsletter list.

My goal is to send one email per month, but it's likely you'll get two in one month and then zero for several months as I typically only send them right before a release, announcing a book is coming, and then right after, with buy links to each retailer.

Thank you,
Jana

Made in the USA
San Bernardino, CA
31 July 2018